THE LAST ALEURIAN

NECROMANCER'S FOLLY

DREW R. STOWELL

EMPEROR BOOKS

Necromancer's Folly

Copyright © 2025 by Drew Stowell

All rights reserved.

Published by Emperor Books

Bellerose Village, NY

Library of Congress Control Number: 2025927747

ISBN

Digital 978-1-63777-681-0

Print 978-1-63777-682-7

No part of this book may be reproduced in any form or by any electronic or mechanical means, including information storage and retrieval systems, without written permission from the author, except for the use of brief quotations in a book review.

Contents

Prologue	1
1. First Encounters	7
2. The City State Edren	28
3. Shock and Preparations	48
4. Revelations	67
5. An Unexpected Mission	78
6. Husks	100
7. The Mad Scientist	111
8. Is this the end?	138
9. Meetings	153
10. Teams	170
11. Lost Light	181
12. Tomb of the Fallen	194
13. Treachery	215
14. Lord of Edren	238
Epilogue	250
Glossary	257
About the Author	267

I've dedicated this book to Markaye. She was someone I looked up to and knew would always be there for me. I miss you Grammy.

"Total war breeds discontent on all sides. Those who participate in such warfare may soon find themselves at the mercy of both friend and foe alike."

- General Wolfram Tors, Commander of the Third Imperial Army of Aleuria

FULL TALMARA MAP

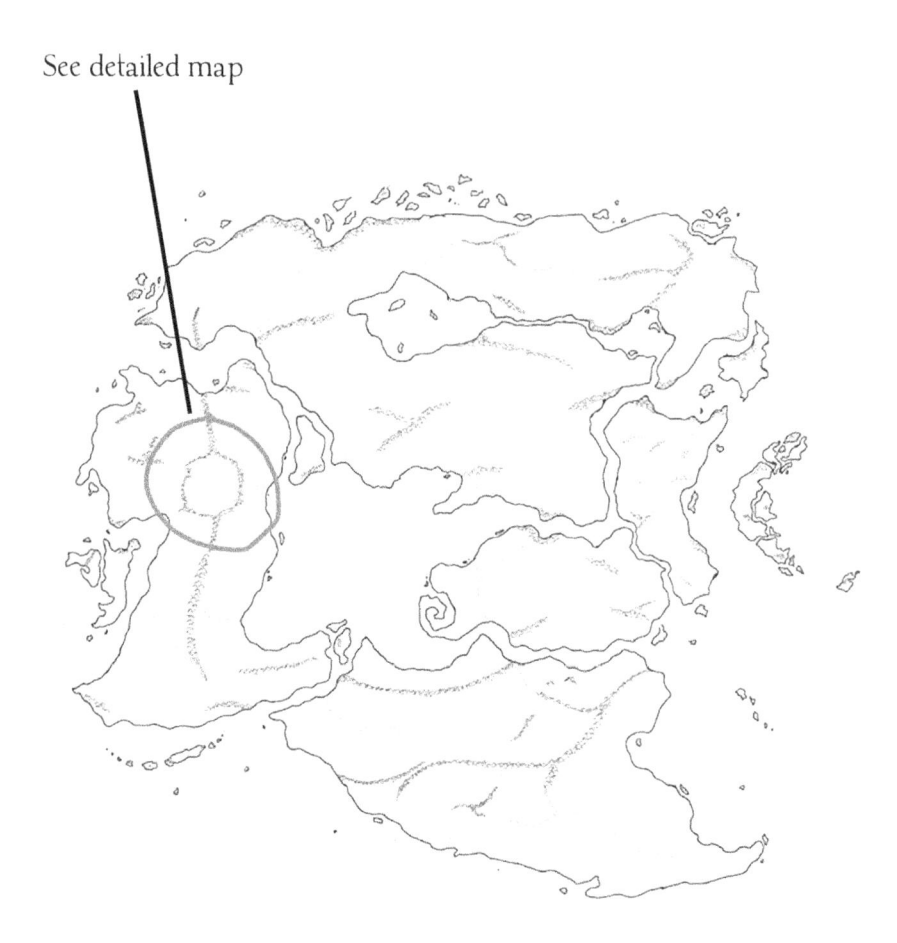

See detailed map

VALTION SILMA CITY STATE ALLIANCE

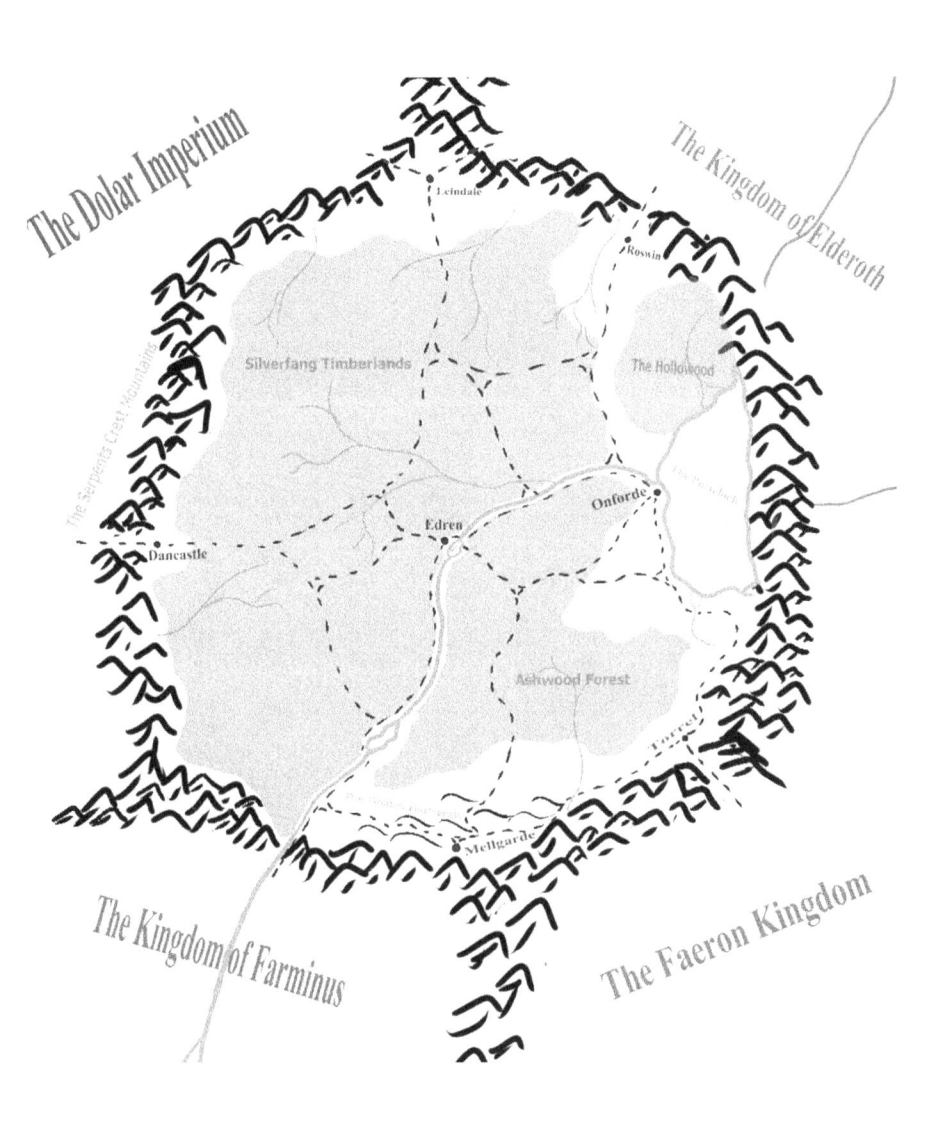

PROLOGUE

Kyrtvale – near the third exit.

The sounds of combat rang out amongst the grand, open landscape of Kyrtvale. Metal against metal echoed through the blazing wastelands and between the frozen pillars of ice; cutting through the raucous screams of tortured souls, a choir of the damned.

A resounding roar echoed across the fields of bones, causing even the leather-winged creatures and multi-headed denizens of Kyrtvale to cower instinctively.

The source of the sound was a beast of immense size.

Its lower half was that of a hairy beast. The knees were backward compared to that of a human and where feet should have been, were instead large hooves reminiscent of a goat or ox that took their place.

The torso and arms of the creature were covered in pale flesh and rippling muscles. In one hand was a massive greatsword of black metal, which resembled the height of a full grown man.

"What's wrong? Didn't you say you would crush me like an ant?"

The taunt came from a man standing nearby, his odd blade at the ready. He was about six feet tall with dirty blonde hair and dazzling sapphire blue eyes. His once nice clothes were worn and tattered in places, his white longcoat was open in the front revealing a coat of mail peeking from beneath a ruined blouse.

"You impudent little thing! How dare you do this to me!"

The beast's beady black eyes were bloodshot with rage. A torrent of boiling crimson spilled from between its fingers as the beast held onto its severed horn in pain; each drip on the black stone beneath it resulted in an audible sizzle.

The man smirked, "I don't see what the issue is. You still have another one, don't you?"

"Do you know who I am!?" The beast ground its teeth as it seethed, **"I am the guardian of the third exit! I was appointed by Lord Atre himself to guar-"**

"Yeah, Yeah. I heard you the first time," the man interrupted without an inch of fear in his demeanor, "And just like the first time you said it; I still don't care."

The beast squinted its eyes at the man.

"You..."

The man lunged forward toward the beast, not allowing it to finish its words. Yet, the beast was ready. It flung a hefty backhand at the man, knocking him to the side with a grunt.

The man, undeterred, rolled back to his feet and pressed the attack. The large black metal blade swung in a wide horizontal arc, forcing the man to distance himself from the beast.

At this moment the creature arose from its kneeling position, its height nearly double that of the man's.

Prologue

Why do they always have to be so damn large, The man thought with an audible *tsk*.

"You're a quick little bug, I'll give you that."

The beast snarled.

"No matter. You will eventually tire yourself, then it will be all over."

It readied its blade in front of it as it spoke, pointing the tip of the great weapon toward the man.

The man dropped into a lower stance as he prepared to strike, all of the possible angles of attack rushing through his mind.

With a smirk, he spoke once more.

"Are you sure you can survive long enough?"

Without missing a beat, the man tightened the grip on his sword and launched himself forward at high speed.

"I only need to hit you once!"

The great beast swung its weapon once more in an attempt to bisect the man, but he saw it coming. The man jumped to avoid the low swinging blade, only to realize at the last moment that this was what the beast had wanted.

The black blade's trajectory was reversed as the beast went into a backswing.

The man forced his back muscles to contract just in time to see his reflection along the polished weapon as it nearly took off his nose. He took the dodge into a backward roll to regain his footing.

"Hey, that's dangerous," The man joked to the bewildered beast.

But even as he joked, his mind was abuzz with tactical assessments. He knew that the beast was intelligent, but he had underestimated it. Leading your enemy into a false attack was a level of tactics he had not believed the beast possessed.

The beast let out a furious roar which shook the very air itself, but the man wasn't intimidated. He had spent much time in Kyrtvale, far too much for his liking. However, during this time he had learned much about the creatures that called it home and was forced to steel himself against their fear mongering.

With the beast's horn forward it charged at the man, intending to gore its opponent. The man countered the beast's rapid approach by charging toward it himself.

If I time this right... The man thought but a moment before springing into action.

Just before the two collided, the man dropped to the ground and slid beneath the beast as it charged and delivered a heavy strike across its abdomen. A loud hiss sounded as its boiling blood splashed upon the darkened stone below.

A pained howl was released from its mouth as it clutched its stomach in pain and desperately swung its blade behind it, but the man was no longer there.

"You know, I did tell you I didn't want to fight. You brought this on yourself."

The beast turned its foul body toward the man, who was standing at the ready just out of striking distance. The two of them began to circle around a middle point between them, each ready to strike.

"Lord Atre warned me about your people."

"Oh yeah? What exactly did he say about us?"

"He told me you Aleurians are a tricky bunch and I should never let my guard down." The beast spat.

Prologue

"He isn't wrong about that."

"He said that to let any more of you escape would be a disgrace worse than death."

The man paused at the beast's words.

"What do you mean by that?" he demanded, "More of my people have escaped?"

A smile grew across the beast's hideous face.

"Maybe, maybe not. It's too bad you won't be around to find out!"

With that statement, a massive ball of twisting flames and scorching heat emerged from the beast's mouth that encompassed the man and everything around him.

"RAHAHAHA!"

The beast let out a bout of deep laughter with echoed across the open air. As the flames dissipated, only ashes remained.

"Serves that little worm right!" The beast boasted, **"None could go against my power! RAHAHAHAHA!"**

The sound of someone dusting themselves off appeared from behind the beast as it laughed joyously.

"Well, that was unexpected."

The beast froze; Its laughter stopped as it slowly turned around with wide eyes.

"H-How!? How are you still alive!?"

The man he thought had been incinerated was instead standing before him without a single burn. His clothing hadn't even been singed.

The man smiled.

"My turn."

He rushed forward with a speed greater than even the

5

beast could muster. Taken off guard, the beast did its best to pull its blade up in time to block, but it was not meant to be.

The man's blade found the beast's neck and its head toppled from its shoulders, landing upon the ground with a wet *Thump*. The body soon followed.

"I know this is a little late but," The man approached the beast's severed head, "You really should have listened to your master."

But the man was right, it was too late. The beast had died without hearing the man's advice.

The man let out a loud sigh, "Really? Fire breath? What kind of sick joke was that?"

He wiped the blood from his blade and, after a quick inspection, returned it to its scabbard at his hip. He had never expected the beast to have such a card to use, yet he took it as a learning experience. It was yet another example of how much was left to learn.

The man approached the severed horn that lay upon the ground and placed his hand above it. A moment later, it disappeared as if being sucked through a whirlpool in the air. He did the same thing with the beast's black sword as he never knew if it would come in handy at a later point.

"Anyway, now that it's dead..." The man looked to what they had been fighting over; A precariously carved staircase in the side of an impossibly large mountain.

He was intrigued by what the beast had told him. Had more of his people really made it out? Or was it just a trick to get him to lower his guard? Regardless of which one it was, he knew he wouldn't find out more by staying in the land of the dead.

With that thought, he started climbing.

CHAPTER 1

First Encounters

I had no idea how long it had been since the battle at the base of the mountain. Hours? Days? Weeks? It did not matter to me, for I could see the light at the end of the tunnel... literally.

"Almost there," I told myself.

The steps carved into the mountain were numerous, but they eventually transitioned into a steep tunnel that pierced into the hard rock face. Much time passed on the journey up, but as I was near despair, I could see a faint dot of white ahead of me.

The sight of that alone sent a wave of relief through me. I sped up, desperate to make it out of that hellhole.

Once I reached the light, I jumped into its warm embrace, my face hitting the soft earth below it.

Grass! Real grass!

Oh, how long had it been since I felt the sensation of grass on my skin, the smell of damp earth, and the pleasant sounds of chirping birds?

I let myself lay there for a while longer, absorbing everything the world could offer.

After some time, I opened my eyes and got to my feet. Now that I was back in the land of the living, I could enjoy these feelings anytime I wanted. For now, though, I needed to survey my surroundings.

"Hmm... where am I?"

I mumbled to myself as I took in the sights around me. The forest around me was filled with picturesque scenes of nature. Light filtered through the canopy like the backdrop of a painting; the foreground was filled with artful strokes in the shape of trees. The entire landscape was like an artist's canvas.

Behind me was a small hole in the side of a hill, partially hidden by rocks and foliage. A chilling sense of dread radiated from the gape, making it the only blemish on the beauty of the surroundings. It was hard to believe that horrible place was hidden within such a beautiful grove.

"Goodbye, Kyrtvale, It wasn't a pleasure"

I uttered a final farewell to the horrible place I had just come from and set off in the opposite direction from it. My goal was to get as far from there as possible.

As I trekked through the woods, I took in the sounds of nature that emanated from all around me.

Ah... it's so nice. I haven't heard such wonderful sounds in.... wait, how long has it been?

I began to run back through my memories. Time in Kyrtvale was hard to gauge since there was no day or night there, only an oppressive red light that pressed down on you from a crimson sky. I had no way of gauging how long I had spent in the Underworld but judging from how many times I slept, it had been a few years.

And that was okay with me. I had accepted that things

would be very different if I ever made it out. Everything I once knew was gone; it was just something I had to accept and then move on.

So that's what I decided to do. Dwelling on the past would get me nowhere in the new world.

"All right world, bring it on!" I shouted into the forest, causing the birds nearby to anxiously fly out of the nearby trees.

Maybe I had been too loud, but oh well. I was just excited at the prospect of exploring a brand-new world. For a long time, my life had been all about defending myself from the creatures that prowled in The Vale and trying to survive day by day. Now that I was out, I had the opportunity to change all of that.

First things first. I needed to get my bearings.

In order to accomplish this, I found the tallest tree I could and began to climb its slender trunk.

It wasn't long before I made it to the top and was able to peek above the canopy.

As soon as I did, I was enchanted by its beauty. All around me was a sea of leaves, gently waving in the breeze with a backdrop of tall grey mountains whose snow-capped peaks stretched above the clouds.

I took in the wonderful sights as I peered along the tree line for any sign of civilization. After a moment I found what I was looking for.

Several thin plumes of smoke were rising above a grey structure of some kind to the northeast. From the sheer size of it, I was sure that it resembled the wall of a city, but I would need to get closer to be absolutely certain.

"That looks like as good a destination as any."

With a goal in mind, I clambered back down the tree and began to walk in its direction. I figured it would take a day or more to reach it. If I went full speed, I could make it there much faster, but I wanted to enjoy the peace of nature for a little longer.

Soon after, I spotted a bush covered in bright blue berries. As I approached it, I found they gave off a slightly sweet scent. They didn't look like any of the poisonous berries I knew about so they were probably safe.... Probably.

I grabbed a few and popped them into my mouth. At first, it was slightly bitter on my tongue, but then the aftertaste sent a wave of sweetness through my mouth, reminiscent of blueberries preserved with sugar.

I waited a moment to see if there were any strange effects but nothing happened, so I ate another handful. The Vale, short for Kyrtvale, is very scarce in its selection of food and most of it was pretty gross, so having something sweet like this nearly brought a tear to my eye.

They were actually so good that I wanted to take some more with me. I grabbed a pouch from the bags on my belt and stuffed it with as many berries as it could fit.

I tucked the pouch away where I knew it would be safe, and tarried on.

Around two hours after snacking on the berries, I came across a creek lazily winding through the forest floor. The crystal clear water enticed me to take a break.

First Encounters

I put my hand in the cool water and scooped a handful. As I sipped, the water soothed my dry throat, and I found myself drinking straight from the creek.

Despite what people thought, water did exist in The Vale. The problem came the moment you saw it. The water was a murky reddish-brown clay-like color and the taste was horrible. Imagine the worst mug of beer you've ever had, remove the alcohol, and multiply it by ten.

Needless to say, the water from this creek might as well have been ambrosia, the elixir of the gods.

I pulled out my waterskin, a tool that had been neglected in the Underworld, and filled it with water for the first time in ages. I had never once used it to collect water in The Vale but despite how long it had gone without use, it still held water as good as the day it was made.

After savoring the water for a moment, I looked at my reflection. My visage was a shadow of its former self. My hair was long and matted, my face covered in an unruly beard, and I looked like I hadn't slept well in years... which indeed I hadn't.

"I'll need to do something about this," I said to myself before pulling out a small knife and beginning to tame the jungle of hair attached to my head.

It took some work, but it was well worth it. My reflection now showed the dignified face that had been buried for so long. My short, dirty-blonde hair now carried a sense of importance and my sharp features were no longer hidden.

It's not like I never shaved while in The Vale, I just didn't have too many opportunities to do so. But now none of it mattered, the feeling of freedom was truly sweet.

Afterward, I ended up taking a moment to sit at the edge of the creek and take in the atmosphere.

The gently rushing water, the leaves swaying in the breeze, the occasional chirp of a bird. All of these sounds were pleasing to the ear.

"I really needed this."

Just the act of immersing yourself in nature is very therapeutic. I could feel all my stress melt away in the presence of the forest.

After some time, I took another sip of water from the creek and got back to my feet.

"Well, I still have a ways to go so I should get... huh?"

As I was trying to convince myself to get back to trekking through the woods, I felt a presence. It was watching me.

I quickly turned and locked eyes with my watcher. It was a creature around the size of a bear but much leaner. Its fur was black and grey with dark, bone-like growths coming out of its shoulders and back.

Through the bush that slightly concealed it, I could see more of those bony protrusions sticking from the back of its paws, and they didn't look very nice. A dried red substance stuck to them and I was fairly certain they were super sharp.

Its low growl was accompanied by the baring of white fangs.

"Oh?"

I couldn't help myself. It had been so long since I had seen a wolf, and this beast was a step above that.

"Are you here to play with me?"

I couldn't help but smile at the creature while looking deep into its eyes. The beast took a step back, seemingly unnerved by my lack of fear.

First Encounters

Then, it bolted in the opposite direction from me.

"Hey!"

I called after it.

"Looks like it wants to do this the hard way."

I chased after the beast, fully immersed in the hunt. It was my first "normal" beast in a long time, so I was excited to see how strong it was.

Man, this thing is fast.

The beast was running at a speed that defied its size but made more sense when you think about its wolf nature.

This wasn't a problem for me though, I was able to keep up with it through the forest, dodging between trees and over rocks, never letting it out of my sight.

"Running will only make it worse."

The beast turned his head around and let out a loud whimper when he saw that I was just behind him. His self-preservation instincts must have kicked in since his speed continued to increase.

"I'm not going to let you go!"

Despite my shouting, the beast seemed set on running with all its might. I couldn't help but admire its tenacity. The burning desire to live is one I was intimately familiar with.

The beast dodged behind a rock in an attempt to lose me, but I flew right over it to the other side.

"Huh?"

The beast wasn't there.

"I'm sure it went behind this rock...."

I inspected the rock but it was just a normal boulder, just like any you could find in the woods.

"Where could he have-THERE!"

I spotted the beast not far, running through the trees. It seemed to have thought it lost me, but it wasn't that lucky.

The wolf let out another whimper, then a growl as I drew near it once again. I could tell it was getting tired. Every moment that passed, its speed was decreasing.

Soon, I would catch it.

Then, the beast changed course to head towards a large beam of light, a clearing devoid of trees.

I wasn't sure what reason it had for doing this, there was no way to escape in a clearing. Maybe it wasn't thinking anymore and had simply let instinct take over.

The beast leaped into the clearing, gaining some air at the same time, but I was right behind it.

"I have you now!" I drew the blade from my waist and struck the back of the beast. The steel bit deep through the hide and into its flesh, severing the spinal cord.

The beast let out a final cry of pain before hitting the soft dirt with a thump, slowly bleeding from the wound, and was no longer conscious.

"That was a lot more fun than I thought it would be" I mused to myself

I now stood over the beast, contemplating what to do with it when I heard a voice from behind me.

"WHAAAAT!?"

In the forest – near Edren

"Hyyaaah!"

The tip of a broadsword slashed through a small, grey-skinned creature. It was about the size of a dog, with six muscle-bound legs, each with a six-fingered hand where the feet should be. Its leathery skin of dark grey had patches of matted hair across it; bits of unknown flesh and refuse caught within. Its face was a horrid sight, like a bat mixed with a hog. It had large, beady eyes of the darkest black, tall ears that ended in a point, and sharp rotted teeth made for tearing flesh. This was a creature known as a Grell.

The owner of the broadsword, a man wearing partial plate mail with an open-faced helm, pulled his blade back with his right hand, pushing forward a kite shield in his left.

Surrounding him were five more of those disgusting creatures.

"Myrril!" The man called out with urgency, "A little help here please!"

A timid-looking girl with dark shoulder-length hair responded.

"S-sorry!"

She held up a wooden staff topped with a dull red gem, pointing it at one of the Grell.

"*Fire Arrow!*"

The moment she finished speaking, a beam of flickering flame shot from the gem atop her staff and hit the Grell square between its eyes.

The smell of burning flesh permeated the air as the creature fell to the ground in a lifeless slump.

"Nice Shot!"

The man in armor yelled back to the girl, Myrril, at the same time as he swiped at another Grell. The little creature was normally nimble, but the shock of seeing its comrade's head burst into flames caused its reaction time to dull.

The man cut down the hesitating creature before turning

toward the remaining three. Their eyes were now filled with hatred.

"R-Reginald! W-what do I do now!?"

The raven-haired girl's voice was filled with panic as the Grell picked her out as the weakest link.

"Gakgakgakgak!"

The Abnormals let out a horrible laugh at her panic.

"Just keep shooting!" The armored man shouted as he ran towards the Grell.

"*Fire Arrow! Fire Arrow!*"

Two more beams of flickering red light shot toward the Grell as the armored man approached from behind. The first Fire Arrow missed its target at the same time as the armored man's blade bit into the back of one of the creatures.

The second arrow hit a Grell in the chest as it stood upon its back legs, causing it to drop the large rock it had picked up and attempt to pat out the flames in a panic.

The armored man wasted no time in the confusion and cut down the remaining two Grell, sending their putrid souls back to whatever hellscape they came from.

"You okay?"

Myrril was now on her knees, breathing heavily. Reginald was concerned about her, but he also knew this was normal.

"Y-yeah... I-I'm um... I'm okay...." She replied in a small voice.

Reginald swiveled his head, inspecting the area around him. He was sure that was the last of the Grell, but you could never be too careful.

He looked down at his comrade on the ground.

"You take a moment to catch your breath, I'll grab the ears."

Myrril nodded in response.

Pulling out a dagger, Reginald started to remove the slightly pointed ears from all of the Grell as proof of extermination. It was a strange thing to do, but it made sense. They were being paid to kill Grell; it was only natural that their client would want proof that the job had been completed.

Reginald put the last of the ears into a leather pouch and turned back towards Myrril.

"You ready to go?"

Myrril was now standing, leaning on her staff for support, her robes covered in dirt.

"Mhm," she nodded.

Myrril was a timid girl who tended to get panic attacks after combat. This caused her to have bad experiences working in groups. But despite this innate flaw, she was pretty good at magic.

Reginald led the way with his shield out front, while Myrril followed behind him.

They weren't too far from the city, but it was always a good idea to be cautious in these woods. If you were unlucky, you might run into creatures such as Arache or Rokrol, though this was fairly rare.

About half an hour later, Reginald suddenly stopped and drew his weapon.

"W-what is it?" Myrril stuttered.

They had just entered a clearing when Reginald stopped them.

"Shh." He replied in a hushed tone, "I hear something approaching."

A chill went up Myrril's spine. Her heart started beating faster and faster, the sound of blood thumping in her ears.

One moment, two moments, three.... Then, the rustling of bushes was heard to their left.

They quickly repositioned themselves with Reginald facing the source of the sound and Myrril behind him. Their rapid response was proof that they had done this many times before.

The second they got into position, a mass of black and grey burst from the underbrush toward the two.

Its massive form was complemented by long white fangs and sharp claws. Bony protrusions graced its shoulders and back. The creature itself was letting out a deep growl.

"DIREWOLF!!!"

Reginald shouted as he moved his shield above them to block the leaping animal.

All time seemed to slow down.

A shrill scream came from behind Reginald as Myrril finally registered the beast.

In but a moment's time, Reginald knew this would be an impossible fight ahead of them. Direwolf jaws were strong enough to tear through a heavily armored knight, their hides were thick enough to deflect crossbow bolts, and they were much more agile than their size would imply.

The ultimate predator.

...

....

"I have you now!"

With an unfamiliar voice came the sound of a blade biting flesh, an animalistic cry, then a thumping sound.

"That was a lot more fun than I thought it would be."

The unfamiliar voice spoke once again, this time allowing Reginald and Myrril to hear the strange accent.

This prompted Reginald to peek over his shield, but what he saw sent him into a state of shock.

"WHAAAAT!?"

He couldn't help but let out a confused cry. Standing over the body of the Direwolf was a single man. He wore a worn longcoat and wielded a strange blade in his right hand, about the size of a longsword.

It was completely absurd that a man wearing no armor managed to kill a Direwolf in a single strike with a steel blade. No, the fact that the man struck the beast while it was in a full sprint was even more absurd.

"Huh?"

I looked behind me in order to locate the source of the confused voice and found that I wasn't alone in the clearing.

Standing not far away was a man holding a shield in one hand and a broadsword in the other. His polished plate armor and open-faced helm were covered in micro dents and scratches, evidence that it was well used.

Behind him was a woman who seems to have fallen to the ground. She sat there clutching a staff affixed with a dull red stone, shaking profusely.

Is she... hyperventilating?

"Um.... Is she okay?" I decided to ask the man.

He glanced at her for a moment before returning his gaze to me.

"Who are you? Where did you come from?"

He kept holding his shield in front of himself while throwing questions at me. Strangely enough, I wanted to ask him the same thing. I didn't sense their presence at all while chasing the Direwolf, but now that it was dead I could feel faint energy emanating from them, something almost unnoticeable.

"Mm," I wiped the blood from my blade and returned it to its scabbard.

"My name's Elric," I said with a respectful nod, "And you are?"

The man seemed taken aback by my willingness to answer. He lowered his shield a little bit and narrowed his eyes.

"I'm Reginald," he motioned towards the woman on the ground, "This is Myrril."

Through all of this, the man never broke eye contact with me. He was being very defensive, but that only made me more curious.

"I'm not a bandit if that's what you're thinking."

I decided to throw that out there to gauge his response. How he reacted would help me determine my next course of action.

"If you aren't a bandit," the man, Reginald, started, "then just who the hell are you?"

Didn't I just tell you who I was? Oh, I guess he means to ask why I'm out here.

"Are you with the Association?" He asked.

Huh? The Association? What's that?

I shook my head, "I don't know what 'Association' you speak of."

Reginald's face showed confusion at my statement.

He used a finger to tap a small circular badge or medal of sorts affixed to the left side of his chest plate. It looked like a pair of folded wings in the center of a circular border that had some kind of writing on it.

"This one, the Wensworth Association."

I shook my head, "Sorry, no clue."

"How do you not know about the Association?" he asked.

Should I just tell them or should I stretch the truth? Eh, I'll just stretch the truth a little bit. It's probably safer that way.

"I've been living in isolation for a while so I'm a bit behind on the goings-on of the world."

"I see..."

Reginald slowly moved from his defensive posture and put away his weapon. I was glad to be making progress, though I was a bit concerned that was all it took to convince him.

The woman, Myrril, seemed to have recovered from her shock at this point and was now hiding behind Reginald. When she moved, I noticed a medallion hanging around her neck that looked identical to the medal Reginald had shown me.

"You don't have to hide," I called out to her, "I mean you no harm."

This only seemed to make her withdraw even more. Then, Reginald spoke up.

"Don't mind her, she's just shy."

His tone had done a complete one-eighty. He was no longer being defensive and seemed more curious than anything.

"Now then, may I ask you another question?" he inquired.

"Sure."

He pointed towards the fallen Direwolf, "How did you do that?"

"With a sword," I replied, confused.

Reginald shook his head, "No, I mean. How did you kill it in one hit?"

Ah! Now it's starting to make sense. I thought that by his armor he was a well-known warrior, but I suppose not. Maybe he was the son of some noble?

"I've had some practice fighting Direwolves. The key is to aim here, just behind the largest bone on their back, see."

I pointed at the spot I cut, "This spot is their weak point. If you manage to sever the spine, they can no longer move and their organs start to fail. It's practically a guaranteed kill."

"Really?" Reginald asked with some intrigue, "I've never heard of this before."

"As I said, I've had a lot of practice."

Tsk. I need to be more mindful of what I'm saying. I have no idea where I am or how long it's been. Actually...

Reginald seemed to be pondering my answer, seemingly satisfied, so I decided to ask a question of my own.

"Reginald, was it? Would you be so kind as to tell me the current year? I'm ashamed to admit, but I lost track a while back."

"Hmm? The year? Uh sure." He thought for a moment, "It's the first month of summer, year two-hundred-eleven."

Hmm!?

"Sorry, I don't know the exact day," he added.

Reginald must have seen my reaction and thought I was disappointed by his inability to answer.

"Oh, that's quite all right," I quickly replied, "But I was just wondering, you are using the imperial calendar, yes?"

"Of course." He responded with a tinge of confusion.

Wait a second... last time I checked, it was one-hundred-eighty-two on the Imperial Calendar.

"Thank you, I believe I understand when I lost track."

This is so strange. I could have sworn I was only in The Vale for one or two years, yet from what Reginald tells me, almost thirty years had just flown by.

"It's no problem, I understand how easy it is to lose track of time in these woods."

So he thinks I've been in these woods? I guess I can go with that from now on. I'll need to find out some more information before deciding what to do. For starters, how does the Aleurian Empire fare...

"Thank you for the information and our nice chat, however, I think it's time I was on my way," I thanked Reginald before leaning over the Direwolf's body and placing my palm on its hide.

I channeled the magical energy within me, my Megin, into the palm of my hand. The air around my hand seemed to ripple for a moment before I willed it to take hold of the Direwolf. Not but a moment later, it vanished into the ripples so fast that you would miss it if you blinked.

"WHAAAAT!?"

This time, it was Myrril who shouted in confusion. I turned just in time to find her pushing into my space. Her face was way too close and her eyes were sparkling like stars.

"What was that you just did? That was magic, wasn't it? What kind of magic? How did you do that?"

I looked to Reginald for help, but he just stood there shaking his head. Apparently, this happened a lot.

I pushed Myrril off of me and to a reasonable distance. "First of all, that was way too close."

Despite being pushed away, Myrril was still giddy with excitement. It was very off-putting that someone so shy could completely change at a moment's notice.

"Second, all I did was store the corpse for later."

"Store it? How? What spell was that? What affinity? How long did it take you to learn it?"

Her barrage of questions threw me for a loop and I instinctively took a step back before regaining my composure.

"Woah, slow down. One question at a time please."

Myrril took a deep breath to calm herself down before asking me again, "What spell was that?"

The look of curiosity and desire for knowledge hadn't left her eyes, but they weren't as fierce as before.

"I'm not sure I know what you're talking about," I said, "I manipulated my internal Megin to induce a change in the spatial construct of the air around my hand and create a portal-like vortex. Then I sucked the corpse through the vortex and deposited it into a pocket dimension. It's pretty standard, really."

"Huh?"

This process was the usual way to direct magical energy to perform the desired effect in close proximity to yourself.

The fact that Myrril didn't understand what I was saying caused me great confusion.

As if to confuse me more, Myrril spoke up once again.

"Is that a different way to cast spells? I know that some places use different methods but I've never heard of this one before."

"Wait, you're a mage aren't you?" her question prompted one of my own.

Myrril responded with a nod.

"I'm just a little confused here. I was sure the Council of Mages knew all about this method. Hell, they were the ones who invented it."

"The Council of Mages?"

Uh... what? Is this lady messing with me? Nobody becomes a mage without going through the council, much less one with a bloodstone focus. What the hell could have happened...

"So you've never heard of the Council of Mages?"

"Sorry..." Myrril was starting to revert to her normal self at this point so I decided to ask another question before that happened.

"No need to apologize, I'm just a little confused." I started, "If you didn't go through the council, how did you become a mage? And how did you get your focus?" I pointed to the red gem topping her staff.

My question was answered not by Myrril but by Reginald who was, up until now, silently watching the perimeter.

"Hey bud, are you sure you know what a mage is? I don't mean to be rude but with that accent of yours, I assume that a mage is different wherever you come from."

It was only when Reginald mentioned it that I realized he and Myrril had a slight accent to them when they spoke the common tongue, so it was only reasonable that they heard an accent from me as well. Maybe it was some kind of regional dialect?

Maybe because I was taking a while to answer or maybe because he realized what he said could have been taken the wrong way, Reginald spoke up once more.

"Well, to answer your questions, Myrril was initially taught by another mage. Though I guess a mage is really just someone with decent control over Megin."

So it's like a way to describe someone and not a profession? Strange.

Reginald continued, "As for that staff of hers, I believe she got it in a weapons shop. I mean, you can't really cast magic without a focus so they're sold all over."

His last statement caught me a little off guard so I attempted to press further.

"I see, but what I don't... oh," I glanced toward the treetops and realized how low the sun had gotten, "Well, it looks like more time passed than any of us realized."

"I was just thinking the same, "Reginald nodded his head, "We need to start heading back if we want to make it before nightfall."

"B-but I want to... talk more..." Myrril muttered.

I also wanted to talk a little bit more, but it would be too dangerous for them to be out at night. Possibly having sensed our desire to continue talking, Reginald swooped in with a question.

"Hey Elric, where are you heading?"

"Hmm? I'm heading to the nearest town, why?"

"The nearest settlement is the City of Edren and that just happens to be where we're heading," He said with a smile, "Want to tag along?"

Why didn't I think of that? Of course they would be from a town, I could have asked them to show me the way. Wait... did he say Edren?

His request was accompanied by Myrril's shocked face, apparently, she hadn't thought of it either.

If he means that Edren then I should be able to get in contact with the Aleurian garrison there. Though if it's the same city then it raises more questions than answers.

I replied with a smile of my own, "What a wonderful idea, I would be happy to accompany you."

CHAPTER 2

The City State Edren

Taking the lead was Reginald, followed by Myrril, and then me. Together, we began to trek through the thick and untamed woods. Luckily we had plenty of time on our hands and ended up chatting a bit more.

Through this, I learned a fair bit about the surrounding area. According to them, the forest around was called the Silverfang Timberland. It was known for its numerous wolfpacks that occasionally contained direwolves. The Timberland itself spread out across a massive valley encircled by the Serpents Crest Mountains. Cartographers eventually gave it the moniker "Eye of the Continent" for the distinct ring of mountains easily recognizable on any map.

In probing for more information I discovered that a single nation didn't rule this area, but by an alliance of city-states. Edren, the city we were heading for, was one of those members. It also happens to sit in the center of the valley.

The city has the same name and location, so it must be the one I'm thinking of. But a city-state? What happened in the last thirty years to cause this? The Aleurian empire would have to be severely weakened to lose such a strategic position. Unless it wasn't just weakened...

I also learned general information and gossip about the

area. The Dolar Imperium was up to its usual shenanigans; The Faeron Kingdom, which I had never heard of before, was apparently low on food after a harsh winter and was eyeing their neighbor's territory; and a bunch of other useful tidbits i took mental note of.

I also had a chance to chat a bit more with Myrril, who was much less shy when talking about magic.

"S-so, Elric. Um... earlier you said something about a p-pocket dimension?"

"I did. It's a very convenient way to carry things."

"B-but I didn't think something like that was even possible!"

According to Myrril, the idea of opening a pocket dimension had been theorized, but no one's ever been able to do it before.

"Well, I just did it didn't I? I guess that proves it's possible."

"I wish I had a spell like that..." Myrril mumbled.

There's that word again, "spell". This word and other bits of information I've gathered from them contradicted the facts I knew to be true. I believed this indicated that either a fundamental piece of my understanding of the world was incorrect... or I was being led into an extremely intricate trap, but I couldn't for the life of me think of a reason why.

I was just some guy who they happened to run into in the woods. They shouldn't have had any clue about who I was, and I didn't feel as though they were lying. However, there was something off about the whole encounter, but I couldn't quite put my finger on it.

By the time we reached the forest edge, the sun was about halfway past the horizon and darkness was slowly creeping across the valley.

"Wow..."

As I stepped out from the thick forest brush, the sight that came into view caused my surprise to vocalize.

Spread out before us was a field of broken branches and sticks strewn between the trunks of long-dead trees. This area, which resembled a logging site, seemed to stretch far to the left and right, following the tree line around a grassy buffer before the city proper.

A chest-high stone wall accompanied by a ten-foot-tall wooden scaffold sat on the other side of the field. Watch towers cropped up every so often, each manned by no less than two armed figures.

Peeking just over the defensive structure were the very tops of wooden-tiled roofs and stone chimneys, the latter of which had light puffs of smoke emerging from their apex.

"Pretty impressive huh?" Reginald started, "It only offers basic protections, but the upside is that it's easier to move than a proper curtain wall. The city has been expanding a lot lately so they ended up building a bigger wall than they needed."

I understood the logic of such a process. They built a large wall with open space in the center so they could expand inward and wouldn't have to move the wall as many times. Very economical, but the downside is the number of troops you would need to keep watch. Depending on the size of the city, they could be stretching their guards thin to be able to man every tower.

"Though I said 'lately', it's actually been like this for the past two and a half decades," Reginald added with a laugh.

I was genuinely impressed. Moving a wall was no easy task, even one designed to do so. However, his words did raise another question in my mind.

"Does this mean you guys haven't had a war in almost thirty years?"

"Hm? Oh, right. I forgot you don't know much about this area."

"R-Remember we said that... um... Edren is in an a-alliance?"

I nodded in response.

"W-Well this alliance, t-the Valtion S-Silma Alliance, we're in a... um... s-strategic l-location for trade so... It's very..."

"It's a very sought-after place," Reginald jumped in once Myrril started trailing off.

From what I remembered, the valley was large enough to fit a medium-sized country. It was a strategic military and trade location, which is why the Aleurians were so focused on capturing it. Now, this Valtion Silma Alliance inhabited it.

"About fifty years ago we had a pretty large invasion attempt by The Imperium, but they never got this far into the valley."

Myrril nodded along, "E-Ever since then we've had b-border s-skirmishes with them but n-no w-wars."

"I see, so these walls are more to protect against beasts?"

"Yep. Oh, here we are."

I hadn't heard of the Imperium launching an invasion into

the valley, but I had to set the discrepancy aside for the moment. While we were talking, Reginald had led us to the nearest gate, which was farther east than where we emerged from the forest.

Two massive inset doors made of foot-thick logs and banded together with steel reinforcement stood closed in front of us. Each one was slightly taller than the wall, which required an arched walkway above it to connect the scaffold.

To the right of the gates was a massive river several hundred feet away. The crystal-clear water flowed through the immense width of the river and disappeared behind the wall, which ran to the edge of the water, before continuing on the other bank.

"Tsk, looks like we're a little late; They've already closed the gate."

"Does that mean we're stuck out here?"

Reginald shook his head, "No, but the guards aren't usually happy when they have to open those massive doors for stragglers."

I knew what he meant. Back in Tors, the city I grew up in, the guards always complained about how heavy the gate was. Though the ones in Tors were bigger, these still had to weigh several hundred pounds each.

Why don't they have smaller doors next to the gate though?

As I was wondering about the lack of wickets, Reginald called up to the wall.

"Hey! Is anyone up there!?"

After a moment of silence, a head popped over the parapet.

"Who's there?" A grumpy man's voice responded

"Two members of the association and a traveler!" Reginald promptly replied.

"Well, what the hell are you doing out there then? The gate's already been closed for the night."

The man had gotten grumpier as we spoke, probably because he knew what we were about to ask.

"We were delayed by a direwolf in the forest."

"Sucks to be you."

"We request entrance to the city," Reginald continued despite how rude the guard was being.

"Denied. Now go bother someone else."

As soon as he finished speaking, the figure disappeared behind the battlements once more. *If an Aleurian guard acted like this... man, I would hate to see what they'd do to him.*

I had gotten a decent look at the guard on the wall while he spoke. He seemed to be an older man with an uncaring demeanor, which went well with his uncaring attitude.

His armor was a simple breastplate over a padded tunic; Definitely not the armor of an Aleurian soldier.

I turned to Reginald, "So what now? Do we go to a different gate?"

He shook his head, "No, it's too far. We'd likely be set upon by nocturnal beasts."

His statement caused me to raise an eyebrow, which he responded to by saying, "I have one more trick up my sleeve."

Reginald turned back to the wall and shouted once more, "I demand you open this gate before we report you!"

Ah, the old 'Let me see your manager' trick. But will it work?

The old guard appeared once again, "Captain Wicchet won't do shit."

"Maybe not," Reginald shrugged, then he looked back up at the guard with a gleam in his eye, "But I'm sure Lord Aulcrest would like to hear about this."

Aulcrest eh? I'm glad to see that family's still in charge, but going over the guard captain and right to the ruler is just evil!

I could have sworn I heard the guard gulp.

"I-is that right? Well, we wouldn't want to bother the Lord with something so trivial."

The man disappeared once again but nothing happened even after a moment. I turned to Reginald and opened my mouth to speak just as I heard a loud *CHHK*.

The sound of chains followed and a loud creak echoed through the trees behind us as the door slowly opened before stopping with a *Thud*.

"What did I tell you?" Reginald said smugly.

The door was now open just wide enough for us to enter one at a time, but it was indeed open.

We squeezed through the opening of the door and were greeted by the sight of the older guard being chewed out by a much younger guard.

"What's wrong with you old man? Going senile already?"

"T-There were three strange people outside, I didn't want to-"

"Oh save your excuses. I know you just wanted to go nap under the watchtower!"

"No, I-"

"You may be an old man, but you're still a guard. If you can't do even the basics of this job, then you should retire!"

The young guard wasn't letting the older one make any excuses, the sight of which was surreal.

"Don't mind them, Elric," Reginald said as he led us past the two guards.

"Uh, is this normal around here?" I asked with a look of confusion.

"Yeah, " Reginald answered as we continued forward, "The appointment of the guards is down to the Guard Captain. He's generally a pretty good guy, but he's often a little too lax with his discipline; especially when the ones who need to be disciplined are further along in years."

I kind of understood the feeling, but...

"I don't think that excuses a lack of discipline."

Reginald shrugged, "I agree, but I think it has to do with his old man. I'm not sure though. All I know is that they were close."

"Still..."

The idea of a soldier, the Captain of the Guard no less, shirking his duties in such a way was unthinkable in the Aleurian forces. There's no way they would allow this to happen, though I guess I already knew that Edren wasn't in the Aleurian Empire anymore so it makes some sense.

Reginald suddenly stopped and turned to me.

"We need to stop by the Association but you're welcome to come with us."

Myrril looked at me hopefully, "Y-Yes, y-you can sign up with them t-to!"

I was somewhat tempted to do so, but I had my qualms. The way the Association worked was a bit different than a guild. They were more of a gathering place for mercenaries to find jobs and information as well as help with materials and equipment, all for a percentage of the reward.

However, at that moment, all I wanted to do was book passage back to Aleuria and find some more information about what happened. Going on an adventure with these two sounded fun, but I had more pressing matters to attend to. Besides, I didn't want to have my name attached to an organization I knew nothing about.

"Sorry," I shook my head, "It sounds like fun, but right now I just want to find a way home."

Myrril looked disappointed, but Reginald nodded in acknowledgment.

"I hear you."

"A-Are you s-sure?"

"I'm sure."

Myrril hung her head.

"But," I continued, "After I take care of a few things back home, I think I'll come back and try out some freelance work."

She immediately perked up, "Really!?"

"Yeah, it sounds fun!"

Now, we were all smiling. After talking with them through The Silverfang Timberland, I got a good gauge of their personalities. They were good people.

After some more goodbyes, I parted ways with Myrril and Reginald; but not before they directed me to an inn they both liked.

Although it was dark, simple lamps were lit outside of buildings that let me take in the architecture of the city. All of the buildings were one to two stories tall, with the occasional three-story building cropping up here and there.

The materials used to construct the structures were very curious to me. Unlike the buildings I was used to, which were either made entirely out of stone or had a combination of stone-ground floor and wooden second floor, these were nearly entirely made out of wood.

The walls were covered in a light-colored plaster, every window had glass, the roofs were covered in wooden shingles, and the style itself was quite different.

I could admit that the buildings were very interesting to look at, but it still made me a little uneasy seeing how different things were from what I was used to. I supposed that this was how travelers felt when they visited a different country.

The Inn itself wasn't hard to find, and before I knew it, I was standing in front of a cozy-looking two-story building. The sign above the door read 'The Hungry Boar' In white ink. I could already hear the sound of merriment and rambunctious laughter coming from inside.

I pushed open the door, and before I had even set one foot on the cobblestone floor, was greeted by a rush of hot air and wonderful-smelling food. The entranceway was well maintained and nicely decorated, nothing too expensive but still tasteful. In the center of the room was a small reception desk, to the right was an open doorway where all the sound was coming from, and to the left stood a staircase leading to the second story.

"Welcome to The Hungry Boar, how may I be of service?"

The voice came from the man behind the desk. Despite the fairly normal clothing he wore, his posture was impeccable. He seemed to be in his late forties to mid-fifties and his hair was greying.

"I'm looking for a room if you have any available."

"Of course sir," The man looked down at his ledger, "we do indeed have some vacancies. A single bed will be three Silver Sovereign a night."

What the hell is a Sovereign?

"I apologize, I only have Solaires. Will that be a problem?" I showed him three silver coins, each stamped with the image of a sun rising over a mountain on the front and an island on the back.

The man just smiled, "Not a problem, we accept foreign currency here."

I was starting to feel relieved before he pulled a scale from under the desk.

"First I will have to verify their weight, of course."

The way he never broke his smile was a little unnerving but I agreed to weigh the coins anyway, there was no reason not to.

The man placed my three coins on one side of the scale and three of his own silver coins on the other. From what I could see, they were stamped with the relief of someone on the front and some sort of symbol on the back.

After he released the coins, I held my breath. It made no sense to be nervous but I just couldn't help it.

It took only a second of back and forth for the scale to settle down, and what it showed was shocking. The

Aleurian Solaires weighed much more than these Silver Sovereigns.

"Hm," The man seemed slightly surprised as he wrote something down, before testing a single coin on each side. This resulted in the same thing happening.

A few more moments passed as he calculated something behind the desk, then he stood back up.

"It appears that your, Solaires was it, contain twice as much silver as a Sovereign."

He pushed one of the Solaires back and added a single Silver Sovereign.

"Here is your change," He pulled a room key from a drawer, "and here is your key."

"Thank you," The man bowed slightly as I retrieved the coins and my key.

"Before you go, there are a few things I must inform you of."

"I'm listening."

The man nodded, "First, meals are available from dawn till midnight. The kitchen is closed past that. Second, you are free to drink as you please in the tavern but we ask you to leave your weapons in your room or at the door. This is non-negotiable. Other than that, please enjoy your stay with us."

"Thanks," I turned to head up to the room before remembering something, "Oh, I never got your name."

The man smiled at me, "I am Fredrick, and this is my Inn."

"Nice to meet you, Fredrick, I'm Elric."

The man – Fredrick – responded with a polite nod, and I made my way up the stairs and to my room.

It wasn't very large, but it was big enough for my needs.

There was a decent-looking bed next to a small desk that sat underneath a window. There was also a wardrobe on one wall and a set of hanging hooks opposite it. The whole thing was a little cramped, but it worked well for one person.

I removed my coat and sat on the bed. It felt really good. Not the kind of good that a cloud-like bed can give you, this was the kind of good feeling that could only be felt by someone who hasn't slept in a bed in years.

My eyes started to feel heavy so I forced myself to stand. I couldn't fall asleep just yet, no matter how much I wanted to. Instead, I sat at the small desk and pulled out a leather-bound book.

This was a journal I had kept on and off since my fifteenth birthday. I wasn't much of a journal guy, but with how strange this day had been, I felt like I needed to keep track of it all.

"Let's see," I said to no one, "I should probably write down all these questions in my head."

The sound of scratching filled the room as I began to write all my thoughts down in preparation for what was to come.

Kyrtvale – Office of the Overseer

"My Lord! Urgent News!"

A small creature ran down a hallway of obsidian-black stone and didn't hesitate to burst through a large set of ornate doors inset with ghastly images cast in gold.

"This had better be an emergency or so help

me I will not hesitate to throw you off the tallest tower,"** a male voice spoke in a deep and commanding voice which sent the creature into an uncontrollable shake. It was as if the very fiber of its being feared the owner of this voice.

"Speak!"

"Y-Yes m-my l-lord," The creature knelt in front of a massive bone-white desk in the center of the room and began his report.

"There has been another breach, this time from the third exit."

"WHAT!?"

The owner of the voice stood from behind the desk. His black eyes and yellow pupils were trained on the creature. The man's skin coloration looked like a moving thunderhead of deep burgundy and cobalt blue swirling together. Two horns protruding from his forehead curled backward over his slick obsidian hair. Growing from behind his ears were strange, leathery feathers that lay flat on the side of his head. The same feathers could be seen around his wrists, laying down almost like scales. A dagger-like object floated behind him on the end of a long tail.

Other than that, he looked like a human wearing an expensive suit.

"What do you mean the third exit? The previous breakouts happened on the other side of my domain!"

The color drained from the creature's face at his master's outburst; but despite this, it managed to stutter. "I-I'm j-just r-reading the r-report..."

The man sat down with a huff, his tail whipping back

and forth behind him. He placed a hand under his chin as though contemplating his next course of action.

"Seal the third exit and increase the security at the other ones."

"B-but sir, that would seal eight exits now! If we seal an exit every time a soul escapes we wouldn't be able to take in anymore!"

The man behind the desk was slightly surprised at the creature's uncharacteristic outburst, but he didn't let that phase him.

"Do you not think I know this? I assigned a guard to that exit, meaning no mere soul could have made it past. It must have been one of *them*."

"This looks like the place."

It was sometime past morning but not quite midday yet. I had eaten a decent meal at The Hungry Boar and headed out to run some errands. The first thing on the list was a currency exchange.

I figured I would need some local currency since not all places would accept mine. That, and I should be able to double the amount of money I have since Aleurian Solaires seem to use more metal than Sovereigns.

At that moment, I was in front of a large building that handled currency exchanges. I had no idea where one would be, but Fredrick was happy to give me directions. Despite this, I ended up getting lost for a bit.

Let's not get this wrong, the directions were good. It was

the city that was confusing. It looked like multiple separate towns clustered around a decently sized lake in the center, which was then collectively enclosed by a large wall that snaked its way across the landscape.

The center of the expansive wall was a large cluster of tents and temporary structures that formed the central market of the city. To the right of it was the lake and one "town" was to the top and bottom of it. The third block of buildings was across the lake, the only way across being bridges placed at the river entering and exiting the lake.

To the left of the market was the old city. The wall surrounding the expanded city met up with a much taller stone wall nearly thirty feet high which encircled the old city. What was once a bright white stone was now a dull grey and had signs of weathering and patchwork repairs. This was the original Edren, the one I knew; and it had outgrown its original footprint.

I had thought about entering but I ended up putting it off for later. Still, the sight of the wall was both nostalgic and sad. The majestic wall I remembered had been reduced to such a lowly state and it hurt.

I shook the thought out of my head and focused on what was in front of me.

I opened the nice wooden door and walked into the reception area. The room was classically decorated with a brass chandelier hanging from the ceiling and multiple people manning the reception desk.

As I approached, one of the tellers called out to me.

"I can help you over here sir."

I approached the young lady who called out to me. She seemed a little older than me, with bright eyes and a soft face. Her long hair flowed behind her and she gave me a nice smile.

"Hello, I would like to make an exchange please."

"Of course sir, what would you like to exchange today?"

"Solaires to Sovereigns please."

The lady tilted her head in confusion, so I placed a gold Solaire on the counter for her to see.

"May I?" she gestured to see the coin and I nodded.

She held the coin up to her face to get a better look at it and her eyes widened.

"Wha- Where did you get this?"

Now her hands were slightly shaking as she stared at me.

Geez, why does every girl I meet end up shaking? ...Wait, no, that's not what I-

"Is something wrong?"

"N-No," The way she said it made me think something was wrong, "I-I need to get the manager!"

And with that statement, she ran off into the back with my coin.

Not long after, I was escorted to a private room by a different employee. It was a comfortable room with a very soft couch and a small table. Tea was already set out as well as some pastries. It looked like the type of place a high-end client would be taken, which only added to my confusion.

I decided to get comfortable for whatever was coming and took a sip of tea.

"Hm, that's nice."

"I'm glad it's to your liking."

With a soft creak, the door to the room opened and a beautiful woman stepped in, followed by the lady who had been helping me. The woman looked to be in her thirties and had a mature beauty about her. She wore thin spectacles and had her hair tied up in a bun. Her clothing seemed to be a cross between a dress and a suit, but she wore it well.

"Sorry to keep you waiting. I'm Gwyneth, the manager of this establishment."

"I'm Elric, and no need to apologize. However, I would like to know why I am here, is there a problem?"

Gwyneth, the manager, sat opposite me.

"Well, there is a problem with the authenticity of this coin," She held up the gold Solaire.

"I assure you, it's authentic."

A wry smile appeared on her face, "Well, you see. That's the problem."

"Huh?"

"I'm not sure how you got your hands on an authentic Aleurian Solaire, and that's where our problem arises."

"I'm not sure I follow."

It wasn't like it was strange for someone to have a Solaire, they were distributed all over the Empire. It's the standard currency endorsed by the King.

Gwyneth gave a sigh, "Aleurian Solaire's are exceedingly rare. They only ever show up at auction every fifty years or so and are always bought by some noble for an exorbitant price, and they are almost never in such good condition. So the fact that you have one is a problem."

"What? But I thought they were only worth twice a Sovereign?"

"If you just appraise it by material value, then yes. However, the historical significance of these coins means they are worth much more."

Now my head was spinning. *What historical significance does she mean?*

"So, does this mean you won't exchange it?"

She shook her head, "We won't."

I may not have understood much of what she was saying, but I did understand what no meant.

Then she smiled, "We would like to purchase it from you instead."

She caught me by surprise. I should have expected some sort of trick but this wasn't even that.

"What?" I exclaimed, "Didn't you just say the origin was in question?"

"I did, but we also don't have anyone calling for missing Solaires, so it's within reason that it wasn't stolen."

Ugh... Merchants.

I took a deep breath and nodded, "Okay."

"Excellent!" Gwyneth seemed to be happy I accepted, "This calls for a celebration."

She turned to the lady who had been helping me originally, who was standing next to the door with a shocked look on her face.

"Go get us a bottle of wine, one of the good ones."

The lady nodded so fast I thought she would get a headache, then ran out the door.

"Wait a second," I was confused about something she said, "Why are we celebrating?"

Gwyneth gave a small laugh, "Why shouldn't we celebrate? It's not every day that you buy a thousand-year-old relic!"

"Huh?"

Huh?

Wait, wait, wait... WHAT!? Hold on, huh? But... WHAT? That doesn't make... these were only minted... but... no...

I kept telling myself that it must be some kind of joke, but I just couldn't accept it. That single statement was the missing piece of the puzzle. Everything that Reginald and Myrril said yesterday that contradicted what I knew, the slightly different way they speak the common tongue, the changed coins, the size of the city, everything. It could all be explained by the fact that not thirty years had passed... but over a thousand.

My head was spinning and I couldn't think straight, that's probably why I did something really dumb.

"Does that mean I shouldn't flood the market with these?"

Gwyneth's eyes went wide, "YOU HAVE MORE!?"

She looked like she was about to faint and honestly, I felt the same.

CHAPTER 3

Shock and Preparations

Let's be honest here, that information was more than a shock to my system and it took me two whole days to cope with it. That time was a little foggy, but I do remember some things clearly.

Gwyneth and I ended up deciding against selling a large quantity of Solaires at once, meaning I was only able to relinquish a few of them. However, it still was more than enough to make sure I wasn't going to be strapped for cash any time soon.

Afterward, I walked back to the inn in a daze and paid for the whole week up front, which Fredrick seemed surprised about.

"Are you sure sir?"

"Yep, no problem."

Then I mindlessly walked to my room and collapsed on the bed. This is where my memory gets hazy. I went back and forth between staring at the ceiling in my room and drinking terrible beer at the bar. Now that I think about it, the amount of alcohol I consumed might have impacted my memory as well... huh.

I'm not sure when but at some point, I learned about my fatal mistake. I had asked Reginald the date, and it was indeed year two-hundred-eleven, and the year I last remembered was indeed one-hundred-eighty-two. However, the Imperial calendar splits up significant changes with era's

So yeah, the time I remembered was from the first era, and you wouldn't believe what era it ended up being. I'll give you a hint, it wasn't the second era. That's right, IT WAS THE THIRD ERA!

"*How could I be so stupid?*" I thought to myself.

I later learned that the second era was considered the human golden age, or more specifically, the golden age of the Dolar Imperium. This lasted over eight-hundred-sixty years, meaning I've been in The Vale for closer to eleven hundred years; but at this point, an extra hundred years didn't even faze me.

"What am I doing?"

It was early morning on the third day, and the sun hadn't even risen, yet I was awake in bed.

What am I doing? I can't let this break me. I'm still alive, I can still do something.

"That's right!" I jumped from my bed.

I couldn't spend any more time sulking. The beast's words echoed in my head.

"*He said that to let any more of you escape would be a disgrace worse than death.*"

There were more of my people that escaped The Vale! I didn't know how many there were, but I knew I needed to find them. Our Empire might have been gone, but we still had a strong sense of community. I was sure they would be looking for each other as well.

"Yeah! Let's do this!"

I ate a handful of those berries I found in the forest for a bit of sugar and rushed out the door. Behind the inn was a small courtyard with a well, a perfect place to do some basic exercises.

Not even a moment after I entered the courtyard, my blade had already been pulled from my pocket dimension and I had begun some basic movements meant to prepare the body and train the mind.

I took each move in painfully slow motions, tensing my muscles as I did so, not forgetting to breathe. This was a technique taught to me by my father, who learned it from his father, who learned it from his father and so on. It was a technique passed down generations of us Tors, meant to increase your fighting ability and train your muscles to retain the memory of your movement. It was called Motion Training.

It didn't take long for my body to ache, and for sweat to accumulate on my face. This wasn't a basic form that just anyone could do. It took immense concentration and physical ability to last longer than a few minutes. I hadn't trained like this in almost a year; however, I was determined to do it, to grasp the only purpose I could. My family was gone, the Empire I served had long since fallen, and the only hope I had left was that someone, anyone, was still alive.

When I had started training, it was still dark out. The only light that illuminated the area was a faint streetlamp in the distance, but that wasn't a problem for me. Aleurians were gifted with excellent eyesight, meaning we could still somewhat see in the dark.

However, within what felt like no time at all, the sky had lightened significantly and more people began to go about their day. I had just about reached my limit and I sat on the ground hard, out of breath and out of strength.

It was then that I noticed the small crowd that had gathered from the inn and onlookers in the street. Some of them broke out in applause while most of them were talking to each other.

"That was amazing!"

"What was that?"

"I'm not sure, but he was like that since I woke up."

"So he's been going for hours?"

"I guess so."

I was a little uncomfortable with all the attention, but there was no harm in it. No one here could copy the technique without rigorous instruction.

"I'm glad to see you back to normal."

Another voice came from behind me. I turned to see Fredrick approaching with a small towel. He held his hand out to help me up.

"So am I, Fredrick," I grasped his hand and stood up, "I hope I didn't cause you too many issues."

"Oh, not at all," Fredrick replied with a chuckle. "I was just concerned when you came back looking so... depressed."

"Yeah, I had just gotten some bad news. But I decided that I couldn't just keep feeling down for myself!"

Fredrick handed me the towel he had been holding and I used it to wipe off my sweat.

"That's a good headspace to be in. Not many people

could pull themselves out of a rough spot so quickly, I'm a little envious."

What he had said was simply the truth of this world. It took considerable willpower to pull yourself out of a rut, the fact that I was able to do so was astonishing, even to me.

The crowd had begun to disperse by now, and I was downing water pulled from the well.

"Hey Fredrick," I took a break between drinks, "Do you know any libraries or bookstores nearby?"

"Oh? I had figured you for a warrior, not a learned man," Fredrick was apparently quite surprised.

He would be more surprised if he knew how many languages I spoke...

"But I digress," He continued, " I do not know of any public libraries in the city. Most large collections of books are privately owned."

"I see... Well, it was worth a shot," I was a little dejected.

"Don't be so quick to jump to conclusions. I said I had no knowledge of public libraries; however, I happen to know of a store that sells many pieces of literature."

"Really?"

Fredrick nodded, "It's a small shop located inside the Inner District."

I got some more information from Fredrick and then began preparing for the day.

The sun was high in the sky, sometime between dawn and midday, and I was standing in front of the large gate into the Inner District. This was what they called the original city, which was where the city's ruler lived as well as various

Shock and Preparations

members of the bureaucracy, wealthy merchants, and the more well-off citizens.

As such, there was a certain standard required to enter. Luckily, Fredrick had informed me of such, so I was prepared. My shirt, which had been shredded in combat with a Barghest, had been mended; and my clothing was thoroughly washed. I had even spent some time polishing my boots.

I had thought about entering before, but I had wanted to get my money exchanged at the time. Now, however, my goal was inside the old city; and after paying the five silver entrance fee, I was finally in.

This place was a lot different than the other parts of the city. The buildings were all much older than the ones outside, not a thousand years old but still old enough. The people here were also better dressed and many wore jewelry I didn't recognise. Even the guards were better armed and armored, with some wearing sets of half plate not too dissimilar to the set Reginald had worn.

Even the streets were different. The rest of the city was only partially paved, cobblestone streets. They were also pretty filthy with horse droppings dotting the place. The Inner District, however, sported the Aleurian standard streets made of flagstone. They were also kept impeccably clean, almost like they expected to eat off of it. Although the age of the city showed in the weathered stones and aged wood, the crowded buildings that lined the road were very well maintained, as was the road itself. Of course, this was a generalization, but it was clear to me that the people of the Inner District enjoyed a pleasant environment. The only eyesore I could see was the original wall in a state of disrepair.

It had clearly seen better days. There were mismatched bricks in various places, probably patches, while other sections were crumbling to the point of lowering the height of the wall by five or more feet in that area, thus requiring a wooden scaffold to maintain the walkway. There were also wooden braces up against parts of the wall, most likely to add additional support to the ancient structure. It occurred to me that it would have been better in the long run to replace the wall. I had my doubts on if it could defend against a siege engine as it was now, but I also knew how the people felt. Many of them would glance fondly at the aged stone as they walked, children were playing in the streets pretending to be guards upon it as they defended from an imaginary enemy; I knew from that moment that they weren't ready to give up on her.

In the center of the old city stood a tall castle made of grey stone and a red tiled roof. It wasn't terribly big, but it was set on a small hill, meaning it could be seen from anywhere in the district.

That's a new castle, isn't it?

The castle was an impressive sight, but it was clearly much newer than the one that I remembered. Aleurian construction was one of the strongest in the world, but even it couldn't stand the test of time.

I was admiring all of this as I followed the directions Fredrick had given me. I passed all sorts of stores ranging from grocers to artisans and jewelers. I was impressed by the amount of market diversity here.

Then, I saw something interesting. Right at the entrance

to an alley were two guards standing watch. Everyone else seemed to be either ignoring them or only glancing for a moment.

As I approached, I started to pick out voices.

"I thought it was an animal attack of some kind, but now I'm leaning towards possibly a Grell."

"I was thinking the same thing. The area around the wounds looks too sharp for a wild animal, and that's before you mention how much of him has been eaten."

It sounded like two men were discussing some kind of murder scene, one having a much more experienced tone.

"What did the witness who found him say?" The older voice asked.

"They found him like this in the early morning, by which time he was already dead."

"Hmm, this has some of the telltale signs of a Grell attack, but something's bothering me."

By this point, I was close enough to see into the alley and it was exactly what I expected. Two men wearing green coats over light armor and a blade on their hip, one seemed to be in his thirties while the other was no older than twenty-five, were standing over the mutilated corpse of a man slumped against the wall.

Wow, that sucks... Hold on, a Grell attack? Something isn't right...

I didn't want to get involved, but something was bothering me about this whole thing so I hesitated. I guess I stood there for too long because one of the guards started telling me off.

"Oi, there's nothing to see here. Be on your way."

I panicked a little at how suddenly the guard started talking, "Oh, uh sure. I was just a little confused is all."

I turned to walk away when another voice called out.

"Wait! You in the white coat!"

Uh oh.

Behind me, the older man in the green coat had called out while his partner looked just as surprised as I was.

"Um, me?" I pointed to myself.

"Yes, you. Come here for a moment."

This caused the other man to break from his surprise.

"Wait just a second, Frank. What are you doing bringing some random guy into a crime scene!"

"You have much to learn, Khris," The older man, Frank, shook his head in disappointment, "This man here's not just any random person. I saw the way he was studying the scene, not to mention what he just said."

He turned to me, "Names Frank Duncan, this here's my partner Khris Lockemor. We're investigators with the city guard."

His partner clicked his tongue at the introduction while I remained silent, waiting for an explanation.

"You just said you were confused, yes? So tell me, what is it that confuses you?"

I thought about just lying at the moment, but I was already fully in the alley and the close-up look at the body made me even more suspicious. Besides, it's a citizen's duty to inform investigators of information that may help their case.

"Well, I was confused as to how it could be a Grell attack."

Frank nodded along while Khris just snickered, "This

Shock and Preparations

man's obviously been torn apart by Grell. They probably came from the sewer grate over there," He pointed to a partially open grate in the ground a little further down the alley.

I shook my head, "It does indeed look like a Grell attack, but that's impossible."

"Why you-" Khris began to speak before Frank put his hand up to stop him.

"Interesting, go on."

At least one of them is interested so this won't be a complete waste of time.

"Well, usually when Grell attack someone there's a lot more normal cuts and bruises from the improvised weapons they use. Then-"

"Well, maybe it didn't have any weapons." Khris rudely interrupted.

"Maybe, but that isn't all. Grell also tend to bring their prey back to the nest to feast on. They also prefer to keep their prey breathing so they can eat them alive."

"This one obviously didn't have a nest," he replied as a matter of fact.

"That doesn't explain why he was only partially eaten."

"It must have been interrupted when his body was found!"

"Hm, I don't think so. A Grell would just attack anyone else who found them. I've never heard of a Grell running from a single human."

"This was obviously different!" Khris was getting really heated now. It seemed like he was desperate to be right.

I shrugged, "It's possible."

"See? He knows nothing." Khris gave a smug smile.

"However," I continued, much to Khris's chagrin, "I've never heard of a Grell killing a human with a single stab to the chest, leaving the valuables, then returning hours later to eat the body where it was killed."

"Wha-!"

Khris was finally speechless, which was a blessing.

"Oh? And how did you come to this conclusion?"

I was all but happy to respond to Frank's question, "I hadn't realized at first, but the victim had a single stab wound to the chest which emerged out his back. This is where the blood had pooled from. Then there's the fact that he still has his rings and bracelet, which seem to be made of silver and gold. Grell love to collect shiny objects, so there's no way one would ever leave them."

Frank nodded along, "Then how did you know he was eaten long after death?"

"It's simple, the lack of pooled blood in the bite wounds. In my opinion, the man was chewed on post-mortem by some sort of canine."

"Amazing," Frank said once I was finished, "You managed to hit all the things I felt were off with this death."

"I've had some experience with Grell so it felt off from the start. Anyone who's fought them before would know the same."

"Nonsense, you did a wonderful job! What was your name again? I feel you would be a great addition to the team!"

Things had started escalating quickly and I needed to find some way out of it. I helped this time because I just happened to walk past, but I didn't want to make it a career!

Shock and Preparations

"My apologies, but I'm not interested in becoming an investigator, I was simply passing by."

"Khris, you could learn a lot from this young lad here, I think it would be perfect if you two could work together on several cases!"

"W-What are you saying, Frank!"

Yep... he's ignoring me. Oh well, this makes a great opportunity to escape.

"Now all we have to do is figure out who killed him, right young ma- where did he go?"

Just as I thought my detour had gotten me lost, I spotted the sign I was looking for, "Fenon Literature and Poetry".

It was a small building squeezed between two much larger ones. It had a large glass window on the front which allowed me to see rows upon rows of bookshelves in a dimly lit interior.

As soon as I opened the door, my senses were assaulted by the smell of musty paper and dust. Much like what I could see from outside, the building was filled with bookshelves, but what I hadn't seen was a small counter in the back.

I approached the counter and saw no sign of Mr. Fenon, whom Fredrick had told me was the owner of this shop.

"Hello?" I called towards a door behind the counter.

There was a dull *thump* from behind the door, followed by the muffled sounds of cursing and things falling over.

After a moment of silence, the door creaked open. Out of the dark room beyond, a figure stepped out. He was a small man with crazy white hair and large glasses that made his eyes seem bigger than they were. I guessed he was in his sixties.

"Why hello there youngster, I'm Euros Fenon. Are you interested in literature?"

The man had a soft but slightly raspy voice as he spoke, probably from years of inhaling dust and mildew.

"Greetings Mr. Fenon, I was told you had the largest collection of books available to the public and I am very interested in something specific."

"Hm," The man looked me up and down with his accentuated eyes before nodding to himself, seemingly coming to a decision.

"You look like someone who can appreciate works of literature. Very well, what is it you are looking for?"

"Well, this might be a little strange, but I'm looking for information on the downfall of the Aleurian Empire starting from the year one-eight-two in the first era. I'm very interested in history, you see."

Mr. Fanon's eyes somehow grew wider at my statement, which was a surprise seeing as they were already comically large.

"I see, that is indeed very specific," He gave me a large, mostly tooth-filled grin, "But I like a customer who knows what they want. I think I have just the book."

He moved around the desk and started to search through the various bookshelves packed with all kinds of works before pulling out one massive, well-worn book bound in leather.

"Here we are, The Rise and Fall of the Aleurian Empire," He set the massive book, more of a tome, on the counter with a puff of dust, "This one's been in my collection for many years, but I would be happy to part with it for someone so interested in history."

I couldn't help but think about how nice of a man this was. He hardly knew me and yet was happy to sell me a book he apparently held very dear to him.

"It's perfect, how much?"

"Let me tally this up," He made a few references to a ledger off to the side and wrote down the price on a piece of paper before sliding it over to me.

I didn't have that good of a grasp of the economy here, but the amount seemed like a lot. Though, once I considered the amount of time it would have taken to painstakingly copy this tome word for word from the original, I decided that it was a fair price.

I nodded, "I'll take it then."

"Excellent, let me get something to wrap this in."

"Oh, actually. I think I'll take a few more books while I'm here if you don't mind."

"By all means."

I had never seen someone with such a large smile in my life. My guess was that someone buying his books to read instead of collecting them made him genuinely happy.

I started to peruse his collection of books and it was impressive. There were many different books on many different topics and from many different ages. Among those that caught my eye was an encyclopedia of various monstrous creatures written nearly two hundred years ago, a book about various types of plants found in the area, a basic history of the world, and a book explaining the basics of magic and spell craft. I was especially excited about that last one.

Buying all these books together was going to cost quite a bit, but that didn't really matter to me. Knowledge was priceless... and I had a decent amount of money.

Afterward, I was eager to head back to the inn and read some of these books, but I had one more errand to run before that. When I was training this morning, I realized that my sword was in a rough shape. The edge had chipped and curled in some places, among other things.

Unfortunately, I couldn't blame this one solely on combat, it was partially my fault. I hadn't been taking proper care of the blade during my time in the Vale. It's true that I didn't have the proper tools to take care of my blade, but that's no excuse to put off repairs now that I was back in civilization. Therefore, my next stop would be a blacksmith which Fredrick was happy to endorse.

It didn't take long for me to find him since I didn't have to leave the Inner District. I approached the squat little shop on the side of the road. The roof was built at a slight angle, it wasn't flat by any means but it also wasn't as steep as the other roofs in the area. Smoke poured from a chimney in the back of the building and the sound of metal hitting metal could be heard from outside.

Hanging above the door was a sign swinging slightly in the wind. It read "Fergus Weapons and Armor," accompanied by an image of a gauntlet holding a sword.

As I opened the door, a muffled clacking sound could be heard from the back of the shop. A small white thread had been attached to the top of the door and ran across the ceiling, probably attached to whatever made the clacking sound.

Shock and Preparations

The shop was decently sized with sword racks and armor stands lining the walls. Shelves holding shields and piecemealed armor stood in the center of the room and barrels full of weapons sat in various places across the space.

Taking a peek at the armaments, the material varied from high-quality steel to wrought iron. What didn't vary was how well-made each weapon was. Even a Warhammer in the corner, which was essentially just a lump of iron with a stick attached, was incredibly made.

Fredrick did say it was a "one-stop shop for all your offensive and defensive needs!"

Not long after the clackers went off, the hammering came to a stop.

"How can I help you?"

A man appeared behind a counter in the back. He was a nearly six-foot-tall, rough-looking man in his forties with a massive build of pure muscle that showed underneath his rolled-up sleeves and leather apron. A pair of goggles rested atop his bald head which he had very obviously just removed considering the rings of soot around his eyes.

"Are you Kent Fergus?"

"Aye, that's my name but I mostly go by Fergus."

Fergus had an accent that was different from everyone else. I couldn't say that I'd ever heard it before, but it was fairly light, so I couldn't be certain.

"I'm Elric. Fredrick the innkeeper told me this was the place to go for quality repairs."

A smile broke on the man's stern face.

"Ol' Fredrick's recommending me again? How's that old lout anyway?"

It appeared as though they were not just acquaintances, but old friends.

"He's doing well. He's been taking good care of me the last few days."

"Aye, that's just like Ol' Fredrick. Always been good at hospitality, he has."

Fergus gave a light chuckle.

"Anyway, what can I do for ye?"

I unhooked the sword from my hip and placed it on the counter, scabbard and all.

"I'm ashamed to say that I haven't been taking the best care of my weapon," I said honestly.

"Lemme get a look at her."

He picked up the sword and began to inspect the scabbard. It wasn't like some I had seen where it was covered in filigree and wonderful decorations. This was a standard scabbard made of sturdy wood covered in thick leather. The only metal on it was at the mouth and the tip, as well as a few metal bands serving as reinforcements.

Fergus stopped at some of the gashes left in the leather wrapping.

"Looks like you've had to use it as a shield, eh?"

I nodded in response. Using your scabbard to stop an enemy blade or as a distraction happened from time to time as a swordsman.

"Well, the wood ain't too damaged, but it could use some new leather."

He moved on to the hilt of the blade. He inspected the guard, which was by far the most decorated piece on this blade. The slightly curved piece of square metal had light designs on its sides meant to give the wielder a sense of dignity. In Aleurian culture, an unadorned blade was considered low quality so even training blades had some kind of design.

His eyes stopped briefly on the wrapped handle before he finished at the round pommel at the bottom of the hilt.

"Hm, could use a bit of polish... and a new wrap..." He mumbled to himself.

After thinking a moment, then giving himself a nod, he drew the blade from the scabbard without a sound.

The blade widened at the base and near the tip, while the middle was thinner. A wide fuller ran the length of the blade, covered in light designs.

"Good fit," He mumbled, "Now let's see what we're working with... hm, I see yer problem."

He ran his thumb across the edge of the blade, feeling the small chips and curls that had accumulated.

"Well, this here's a blade o' fine quality, I must say. Though I'm a little disappointed in yer lack of care."

A frown had appeared on his face while he looked over the blade in a disapproving manner.

"Yeah," I sighed, "I was stuck somewhere without any proper equipment for a while, though I know it's no excuse."

"That's why yer here, huh."

"I couldn't bear to see my blade like this."

"Well, yer edge is chipped, curled, and dulled in places. That by itself wouldn't be a problem but... ye also have a nice warp in this blade. I'd say she's in dire shape."

I couldn't help but feel down about this. I had been granted this sword by my father when I finished basic training. It's been with me through hell and high water... literally.

As I was feeling down, Fergus gave me a big, if slightly smug, grin.

"That is, she would be if it were any other smith working on her."

I perked up right away, "Really!?"

"Aye, I can 'ave her back in shape with about an hour of work. Though, I'm a wee bit backed up at the moment. Come check back in tomorrow, that's the earliest ill 'ave her done. Three days at most."

I nodded as I internally let out a sigh of relief. I didn't know what I would have done if he said it wasn't fixable. Well, I probably would have gone to every smith in the city to confirm, but other than that I would be at a loss.

Fergus sheathed the blade and set it back on the counter.

"While yer here, why don't ye grab yerself some maintenance tools? We sell them over there. I don't ever want to see you bringing in a blade this bad again."

"Thank you, I will."

"And if yer interested in other gear, have a look around. We've got plenty to choose from. I'll even help size em, free of charge!"

With that statement, Fergus took my blade back to his forge and the sound of hammering could be heard soon after.

I looked at the tools Fergus had pointed to and picked up what I felt I would need. Some oil, cloth, a whetstone, and a small bundle of small tools. I was also pleasantly surprised by a stump anvil for sale. They are these small, curved pieces of steel that you hammer into a stump and use as an anvil. They are very convenient for field repairs. Satisfied, I set one on the counter with the rest of the items I wished to purchase and began to peruse the rest of the shop.

CHAPTER 4

Revelations

After spending all day running errands, I was mentally exhausted. As soon as I returned to my room at the Inn, I dropped the burlap sack full of stuff on the floor and practically jumped into bed. I normally didn't run out of energy this fast, but I wasn't used to all this... socializing. It had been years since I had even seen another person, much less speak with them, so it was draining all of my energy to simply get through the day.

It's like having your entire family over for the Festival held every year at the Winter Solstice. You love them, they're your family, but that doesn't mean you can't have a break from how hectic everything is now and then.

The bottom line was that my head hurt, and the only way I knew how to quell it was some peace and quiet. So what was the first thing I decided to do? That's right, I shut myself in a room which sits over a tavern... Not too smart of me.

So, in an effort to ignore the muffled sounds of rambunctious merriment seeping through the floor, I dug into my pocket dimension and began to pull out the books I purchased.

The first book I opened was "The Rise and Fall of The

Aleurian Empire". This massive tome contained the collected information of Aleurian history spanning from the Empire's origins to its eventual downfall, as the title suggested.

Skimming through the majority of the book, it seemed to be fairly accurate at points, then wildly speculative at others. It appeared as though a lot of missing history had to be pieced together by human researchers, leading me to believe that much of my people's records were lost at some point in history.

The tome spoke in detail about the Meritocracy of The Aleurian Empire, mentioning various noble houses who were relieved of their titles due to incompetent heirs. Even in my time, Humans saw this as strange or cruel. However, this was done as a way to ensure only the most capable people would be leading us at any one time. Although it wasn't without its flaws, It was by far a better system than the feudal castes of the human kingdoms, which were greatly prejudiced against the lower castes; especially if they had greater talent than the nobility.

The book also spoke volumes about the various wars initiated by the Aleurians in order to spread their will and power across the land. As children in Aleuria, we were taught that The Empire was expanding into the uncivilized lands inhabited by those not of the Elder Races in order to spread peace and civility. Later in life, we understood that we were more interested in expanding our own influence and securing our future than we were in bringing peace to other lands, as was standard with any land ruled by mortals. It was the absolute order of the world. If we were not securing our own future, nobody else would do it for us.

Revelations

Of those wars, the one that stood out to me the most was about the invasion of the Aleurians into the territory of Edren in year one hundred sixty-one of the first era.

During this time, Edren was a small settlement surrounded by a rudimentary wooden wall. The people of Edren saw the overwhelming might of the Aleurian army, which had brought siege engines of massive proportions as well as nearly ten thousand armored troops. In comparison, the three thousand inhabitants of Edren were dressed in hides and had little to no combat experience. However, despite the constant onslaught of the Aleurians, the people of Edren would not falter.

The general of the Aleurian army, seeing his enemy's willpower, decided to negotiate with the Chieftain of Edren. The general challenged the Chief of Edren to a one-on-one battle, which the chief accepted, believing it to be the only way to save his people. This was the start of the famous battle between Wolfram "Einheri" Tors, and Godfrey Aulcrest, the Chief of Edren. It was a battle that went down in history, because of the tenacity of humans, but more importantly because of the outcome.

Despite winning the duel, General Wolfram enjoyed the spirit of his opponent, so he spared his life and offered him the position of advisor to the new Aleurian noble who would take charge of the area. Because of this fact, and the fact that Edren was never oppressed under Wolfram, the Aleurian General became an icon for the people and still is even after all this time.

"Interesting," I said to myself as I read, fully entrapped by the pages.

The name of Wolfram Tors was known far and wide, as

was the Battle of Edren, and it was something I had heard for many years from my father and grandfather. I was overjoyed that it has been passed down all these years into legend.

The back of the book is what I found most interesting, though. Starting in the year one hundred eighty-two, a sect of the Aleurian Empire defied the King, resulting in a bloody civil war. This was something I was intimately familiar with, or at least the first half of it. It had begun with the outlying areas of the empire but quickly spread inward. By the second month of the war, however, the fight had stagnated. Then came the Eighth month of the year, when the rebellion staged a sneak attack on the city of Tors.

I remembered it well. I was assigned to protect the city I was born in, along with my older brother and countless other recruits. Seeing as it was the homeland, most of the soldiers were sent to the frontline, my father included.

Then, as if Kyrtvale broke through into our world, a mass of red light overtook the skies. From the outside of the city, a massive army appeared and began to launch attacks on the walls. First with siege weapons, then with men.

We broke into a scramble. We did our best to protect the city, but it was futile. My brother was stationed at the main gate, and my unit was sent to back them up. However, we were betrayed by someone on the inside. Once the Steel Defenders turned against us, we had no chance. By the time I had a chance to look upon the gate, it had already been breached.

My memories grow hazy at that point, but I remember the unit I was in being overwhelmed; all of us bloody and battered. Men flooded through the breach and we were quickly overrun. That was the last thing I remember before waking up in The Vale.

I shuddered at the memories that flooded me of the beginning of my time in Kyrtvale.

Don't think about it, don't think about it, don't think about it...

I forced myself to continue reading, focusing on something else was the best way to push unwanted memories from my mind.

What was written next was entirely new and shocking information. The reason Tors and other cities in the homeland came under fire was that several Aleurian generals betrayed the king and marched on Aleuria.

Not even a month after the fall of Tors, the rebel army reached the walls of Solaris, the home of King Theobald Solaris, and the capital of the Aleurian Empire.

According to scholars, the rebel army bypassed the barrier around the city and quickly entered into bloody combat with the defenders. The king, however, knew that he had only one chance to save his people and had deactivated the barrier to lure the enemy in. It was a success; the entire rebel army occupied the city and all of the enemy generals marched on the royal palace. It was then that the king reactivated the barrier and reinforced it so that no one could escape from the city, turning it into a tomb.

The Battle of Solaris was thought lost to time since the location of the city had long been forgotten. Luckily, a written account of the event by an eyewitness was uncovered which helped researchers fill in the gaps of the final days of the Aleurian Empire.

After the battle, it is said a curse was stricken on the

remaining Aleurian population which caused them to eventually go extinct. Though many historians believe it to be caused by the drastically reduced population, as the Aleurian people married into many families, some of which became human royalty across the land.

Thump.

I closed the book and took a deep breath. It was a lot of information to take in. This book had been written quite some time ago, so some of the information may be out of date, but enough of it was true for me to believe it.

The generals betrayed us? Would that mean... No. Impossible. I won't even allow myself to think of that.

The country of my origin had been reduced to nothing in a mere nine months by the very people sworn to protect it. I had come to terms with the civil war several years ago, but the information of the generals' betrayal was still shocking.

I knew I needed to gather some more information so I wouldn't be caught off guard by anything else. To that point, I grabbed the history book I bought and started to flip through it.

It was a basic book that explained the generalized history and major events across the continent to some fair detail. It gave me a good idea about what happened in the thousand-year gap between the fall of the Aleurian Empire and now.

The book detailed that after the fall of the Aleurians, various human kingdoms cropped up around the old Aleurian territories and began to vie for power against each other. Several countries stood out during this time. The Dolar Imperium, the only human kingdom allowed autonomy during the rule of the Aleurians, was able to seize a large portion of Vestri, the western continent; The Wulong

Revelations

Dynasty wasted no time in taking power over Nordri, the northern continent; and the Xoprusal Dominion who spread tyranny over the inhabitants of Austri, the eastern continent. These three superpowers rivaled each other in every aspect, each determined to become the strongest country in the world.

It was during this time that religion also grew in popularity, as people turned to the gods for guidance during a period named "The Hundred Years of Suffering" which took place just after the fall of the Aleurians. In a shocking turn of events the main religion of the Aleurians which worshipped Aleura, the Goddess of Creation and an Elder God, had nearly died out by then and had since been taken over by the worship of the thirteen Primary Gods.

Another shock was the re-inhabitation of Aleuria, the homeland of the Aleurians, by humans and other races. Then there was the forcible takeover of Dwarven lands, which sent them fleeing into their mountain fortresses. It seems that the second era of the Imperial Calendar was filled with unjust persecution of non-humans, perhaps out of fear or jealousy.

As I continued in this section of the book, my eyes fell on the next line and forced me to do a double take.

Wait... what?

I read and reread that passage ten or twenty times before it finally sank in. The crushing reality of the text caused indescribable feelings to well up within me. Anger. Rage. The feeling of pure hatred. My hand shook, the windows rattled, and the air began to grow heavy.

All the while, my eyes couldn't move from that one sentence. "... Due to the unjust attacks by the Elven people, the nations of the world, along with the church, concluded that the only possible solution was..."

The words repeated in my head, the end of that sentence.

"... complete extermination."

Edren – Lord Aulcrest's Office

"... and the final thing I have to report is about The Imperium. It seems that-"

An intelligent man in well-made clothing was giving a report to the lord of the city when he was cut off mid-sentence.

"I've heard. To think they would be so bold as to lay claim to this city. It's ridiculous!"

The man who interrupted him was none other than the lord himself. Lord Aulcrest was sitting behind a beautifully made mahogany desk. He wore vibrant blue clothing made of fine material; his graying hair was well kept and his beard was trimmed short. He wore very little in the way of jewelry, only a signet ring on his right hand and a wedding band on his left.

"Y-Yes sir, I believe so as well. However, perhaps it would be a good idea to check our records just to double check there is no basis for their claim."

The man giving the report was slightly shaken at his lord's outburst but managed to respond with an intelligent suggestion.

Lord Aulcrest furrowed his stern brow, "Hm. Very well,

it would be best to cover all our bases. I'm sure nothing will come of it, but you may proceed."

With that, Lord Aulcrest waved his hand at the man who then bowed and left the room.

"You can come out now," He called out to the dimly lit office.

"I'm impressed, how did you know I was there?"

A figure emerged from the shadow, seemingly melting from it.

"Hmph, I've been around you long enough to know you're always listening, Zed."

The man called Zed was dressed from head to toe in pitch-black fabric. He wore a long cloak with the hood pulled up as he stood in front of the desk. What little moonlight that came through the window behind Lord Aulcrest illuminated the man, which revealed a polished mask of obsidian covering all features, not even leaving holes for eyes.

Lord Aulcrest trusted Zed greatly despite knowing almost nothing about him. What was known is that he had been an advisor to the Aulcrest family since his father's grandfather. If Zed was here, it was to give very valuable information.

"I have important information," Zed's tone was cold and calculating, "In the near future this country will be destroyed."

Lord Aulcrest was startled by Zed's statement and it took all his willpower to stay calm as the leader of a nation.

"When will this happen? How can we prevent it?"

Zed shook his head, "I do not know the specifics. What I do know is that this country will be destroyed and the alliance will shatter."

Lord Aulcrest slumped in his chair. Never had he ever gotten news quite like this in his entire life. Zed had an uncanny ability to predict the near future, in fact, his ability was what allowed a previous Lord to muster a proper defense against the Imperium fifty years earlier, so he knew it could be trusted.

"I do know one other thing," Zed continued, "The person who will bring about this fate, it won't be you."

Lord Aulcrest didn't know to feel joyous or concerned at this proclamation.

Just then, Zed's head snapped to the window that overlooked the city. His eyes, hidden by the mask, were transfixed in one location.

"What is it?" Lord Aulcrest abruptly stood from his seat, alert.

Zed turned back to Lord Aulcrest, "It's nothing."

The Lord looked back at Zed wearily as he sat back in his chair. It was subtle but he had detected a hint of amusement in Zed's tone, which was otherwise completely monotone.

Zed turned and began to make his way out of the chamber.

"Was that all you had for me?" Lord Aulcrest called to him.

"Indeed. You would do well to heed my words." Zed replied without slowing.

Though, as he made his way through the door, a smile crept across his face.

"So, *he's* finally made it," Zed muttered to himself, "This is going to get interesting..."

Revelations

As fast as the feelings began, they were replaced with those of sorrow, loss, and concern. The faces of elves I had known flashed through my head. I couldn't help but wonder what had happened to them; whether they had met a terrible end or lived their lives in peace.

However, the thing that concerned me most was the unnatural way my emotional state had changed. At the moment that my emotions began to swell, it felt as if they were stopped and abruptly suppressed. The implications of this left me both troubled and utterly perplexed.

CHAPTER 5

An Unexpected Mission

The next week passed quickly. At first, I was weary of the humans, but my mind was changed when I spotted several half-elves in the city. After that, I began to notice more and more of the other races.

Edren had a modest population of around seventy-five thousand within the city, and twenty to thirty thousand in various towns and villages within the territory. Around eighty percent of that is Human, seven percent are Elven or Half-Elven, and three or so percent are Dwarves. The remaining ten percent accounts for members of various other races in small amounts.

Thankfully, the human policy of oppressing other races had started going out of style around three hundred years ago. Some countries still discriminate, but most are fairly accepting of different races. The only exception to this would be Elves, whom the church has declared enemies of the world. As such, Edren is one of the only places in the world that still accepts Elves and Half-Elves, rejecting this teaching of the church. Luckily, I discovered that the Elves weren't entirely wiped out, but their worldwide population is thought to be less than one hundred thousand.

I wanted to do something, I felt an urge to help the Elves

in some way. Changing the minds of entire kingdoms was an obvious fantasy, so I decided on something more doable.

For the rest of the week, I began putting my plan into motion. I researched the laws of the area, searched for suitable land, and decided on a policy.

I would help people fleeing their oppressors find a new life in Edren, the land that accepts those shunned by the world. In fact, I was in the middle of securing a source of stable income when something unexpected occurred.

I woke before dawn and went through my daily routine. I grabbed a small breakfast and serviceable ale before heading to the courtyard of the Inn and beginning my morning exercises.

After about an hour of Motion practice, a group of kids approached me just as the sun began to rise.

"Good morning Master," One of the kids cheerfully said.

"I've told you not to call me that," I looked up at the rest of the kids, "Are you all ready for today's practice?"

They all nodded enthusiastically.

A few days ago, I was approached by a few of the local boys during one of my practices. They wanted me to teach them Motion Training. I refused, seeing as it was a secret technique so difficult you couldn't even do it without being taught. Just watching wasn't enough for you to attempt it.

The kids relented, however, and I finally caved and told them I would teach them the basics of physical training. That's how I ended up training six boys, between the ages of ten and fifteen, every morning for the last few days.

"Alright, get into your stances, and let me see how we're doing."

The kids happily lined up next to each other and dropped into the stance I had taught them. It was a simple stance designed to allow you to quickly move from an offensive to a defensive position or vice versa.

I had the kids move forward one step at a time so I could observe their movement and see if they had been practicing at home like I had asked.

"I'm impressed. You've all shown great improvement."

One of the younger kids piped up, "Yes Master! We practice together a lot!"

"I see. Helping each other can indeed be beneficial in training. Also, don't call me Master."

Next, I had them holding straight branches I had carved to look like training weapons and I started them swinging through the air so they could get a feel for the weight and strengthen their arms.

"What's the first rule of this class?" I called out in the middle of the exercise.

"Never harm another person, Master!" They shouted in unison.

"What's the second rule?"

"Always defend those who can't defend themselves, Master!"

"Good," I praised them, "But who can tell me about the contradiction between these two rules?"

The boys looked confused for a moment as they weren't expecting such a question. It had probably never occurred to them that there was a contradiction. Then, one boy opened his mouth.

"Is it because sometimes people hurt each other, Master?"

"Don't call me Master, and yes that is correct." I began my lecture, "There will be times when you must harm one person to save another or yourself. This is the contradiction between the rules. Now, can anyone tell me the meaning of these rules without this contradiction?"

This solicited silence from the kids. Their faces scrunched as they thought hard about what I said.

"I want you all to ponder the answer to that question. However, in the meantime who can tell me the third rule?"

All of them spoke at once, "Never call you Master!"

"That last one is very important, make sure you take it to heart."

"Yes Master!"

I sighed in defeat. It just seemed like there was no way to stop them now that they had started. It's not that I dislike being called Master that much, but it makes me feel really old.

Though I suppose I'm technically over eleven hundred years old... but that's beside the point.

As I was busy being troubled by how old I actually was, someone approached me from behind.

"Wow, the rumors were true. You really are training kids in the back of an Inn."

I turned towards the familiar voice and was greeted by a man in his thirties with messy hair and a well-groomed man in his twenties. They each wore a tan trench coat over hardened leather armor and carried rapiers on their hips.

It was the investigators, Frank Duncan and Khris Lockemor.

Necromancer's Folly

"Oh, Fancy seeing you here." I couldn't contain my surprise, I hadn't expected to see those two again.

Frank had a big smile on his face, "Hello again, Elric. How've you been?"

"Not bad, but I do have a question. How did you find me?"

It was the one thing I couldn't figure out. There were tens of thousands of people in this city, it shouldn't have been easy to track down one guy. *Though he did say "rumors" earlier, didn't he?*

"Oh, it wasn't that hard actually. There aren't too many blonde guys with a uniquely made white coat and odd accent in this city."

Oh... that's true. I guess it wouldn't be that hard to find me if you searched like that.

"Fair enough, but what I can't figure out is why you're here."

Frank chuckled, "It's actually two reasons. For starters," he pushed Khris forward, "He's here to apologize."

"Apologize?"

"Yeah, I wanted to say I'm sorry for doubting you."

Khris looked incredibly embarrassed and awkward while saying that. I actually felt bad for him.

"You see," He continued, "You were right about that case last week. We did some more digging and figured out what really happened."

He went on to explain that the murder victim had been a wealthy merchant with ties to the underground. During the days before his murder, he had apparently been moving vast amounts of cash from one location to another, almost like he was about to flee from something.

"We ended up figuring out who killed him and was able to catch the guy. He was just hired muscle, but it was good to get him off the streets."

"That's incredible." I was genuinely impressed at the outcome, but Khris didn't seem to take it that way.

"It, well it wouldn't have been possible without you so," He seemed to struggle a bit, "I'm really sorry for saying all those things."

His apology seemed genuine, making me reevaluate him as a person.

"It's no big deal, I'm just some guy off the street. I expected some pushback."

My comment seemed to make Khris relax a little bit, but he still had a pained look on his face.

I turned to Frank, hoping to move on from this.

"You said there were two reasons right? What was the second?"

"That's the more important one," Now he started to look a little embarrassed, "It's a little embarrassing for me to ask you this, but we would like your help."

"Oh..."

Now *that* was seriously unexpected. Did these two think so highly of me after one encounter that they would come to me for help with something?

"What do you need help with?" I asked reluctantly.

I don't want to get caught up in anything, though I suppose this could help ingratiate me with the local constabulary so I might as well hear them out.

"I can understand your reluctance, but this is serious. Another half-elf's gone missing, and this time we have a witness to confirm they've been kidnapped."

Ah, yep. A kidnapping ring is exactly the kind of thing I don't want to get involv- wait did he say half-elf?

I could feel my brow furrowing as I processed the troubling information. The last thing I wanted was to get mixed up in a kidnapping ring, but not helping would go against everything I've been working toward this past week.

"Confirmed?" I asked, "So you have suspected they were being kidnapped before this?"

Frank and Khris nodded, "We believed that the disappearance of elves and half-elves in recent months was the work of an underground kidnapping ring, but we had no proof."

"Elves too?" My agitation was beginning to show in my speech.

Frank nodded solemnly, "Yes, full-blooded elves have been taken as well."

My anger began to swell again. Not only did humans nearly complete genocide on the elves, but they also thought of them as commodities to be collected.

"It's despicable," Frank continued, "The elven people have been through enough."

"It makes me sick to think that people are still treating them like things, "Khris chimed in.

I was glad they shared my sentiment and weren't trying to find the kidnapped elves simply because it's their job.

"What do you need from me?" I asked through gritted teeth.

"Wait, really? That's all it took to convince you?"

I nodded, "I didn't want to get involved at first but once I heard it was about elves, there was no stopping me."

"Well then, excellent. We are going to be tracking down the kidnappers so we might get into a fight."

"We've hired a couple of mercs from the Association for extra muscle, but you should be prepared too."

"Right," I nodded at them and turned to the kids I was teaching.

"Sorry kids. It looks like I can't teach you today so I want you to continue practicing your forms."

The kids looked back at me and then at the inspectors. They all nodded as though they understood the situation.

"You're going to help the investigators fight the bad guys right? Then we'll do our best until you return!"

It was one of the younger kids who spoke up, but all of them voiced their agreement like he was saying what all of them were thinking. They were such good kids.

"Thank you for understanding," I turned back to the investigators, "Just give me a moment to grab my gear."

"All right, we'll meet out front."

I nodded and ran into the Inn and threw open the door to my room. I quickly grabbed what I was looking for, the sack at the foot of my bed, and emptied its contents onto the bed.

After about five minutes I had rejoined the investigators outside the Inn, but this time I was prepared.

"Wow, nice gear. Where'd you get it?"

Frank asked as I exited the Inn. I was in my usual clothing, but this time I had on the armor I bought at Fergus's shop. I had steel greaves covering my boots and lower legs; I wore a chest plate underneath my longcoat, which I still kept open, and my forearms now sported simple metal vambraces and light metal gauntlets. My blade was hooked to my belt as usual.

"A smith named Fergus in the Inner District helped me pick it out."

Another smile crept across Frank's face, "So you know old Fergus? I guess it's a smaller world than we thought."

They led the way and I followed. On the way to the scene of the kidnapping, they explained that they also got their armor and weapons at Fergus's shop. He was apparently a favorite of the town guard for how reliable his products were.

Then, we started to discuss the kidnappings. They weren't all taking place in one area, people were being kidnapped from all over the city. They even somehow take people from the Inner District, which has the highest security in the city.

The only connecting thread between all of the kidnappings is the fact that each person has some amount of elven blood.

"The first disappearance was about three months ago, on the other side of the river. Since then, numerous people have gone missing all over the city."

"And there's nothing that connects all of the victims besides their elven lineage?"

"Nothing that we could find."

"Since they were also taken from the Inner District, is it correct to assume there was no discrimination between social status?"

"That's what we were thinking as well. It seems that

whoever took them only wanted them because they were elven."

I was deeply concerned about this. The only reason I could think of to kidnap only elves and half-elves was some kind of massive trafficking ring that sold them to nobles from other countries. The likelihood of us finding any of them was too low for comfort.

They led me to a small wooden house just outside the Inner District. It wasn't much to look at, but it a had very cozy feel to it. There was a small fenced-in garden in the front and flowers blooming beneath the windows. A warm light emanated from inside. No one would suspect it was the scene of a kidnapping.

"Where are the others you hired?" I asked after scanning the surroundings.

"We sent them to canvas the area," Frank replied, "We'll catch up with them in a bit. For now, let's go inside."

Frank stepped up to the door, knocked twice, and entered without hesitation. I followed behind, with Khris coming in last.

The inside of the home was as cozy as the outside. A warm candlelight filled the interior. The furniture looked decently made but had been worn throughout time. The walls had small knick knacks and books sitting on shelves, and little portraits of people hung in frames.

Just past the entranceway was a sitting room where the owners of the house awaited. One was a human man in his late thirties with dark hair and puffy eyes from crying. In his arms, weeping softly, was a beautiful woman with pointed ears and long blonde hair. I couldn't tell her age, but she looked the equivalent of a twenty-year-old human, so she was still young for an elf.

As the man saw us, his eyes became filled with hope.

"Mr. Duncan! Did you find our boy?"

The elven woman managed to calm herself down at the man's question.

"I'm sorry, not as of yet," As the words came out, all of the light drained from the woman's eyes and she began to cry once more, "But rest assured, we are taking this very seriously, we know that time is of the essence so we brought in someone who has helped us in the past."

Frank gestured to me and I took a seat across from the two. I took a moment to look them over to confirm my assumptions about them. The man gave off a faint sense of Megin, seemingly less than the average for a human.

The woman on the other hand had a light green aura around her, most likely her Megin leaking as a result of distress. All creatures with high Megin capacity have this issue, even the Aleurians. It wasn't thick enough for a human to see it, but it was enough for me to confirm that she was a full-blooded elf.

"Mr. and Mrs. Lux, my name is Elric. I'm here to find your son, but I'm going to need to ask you some questions."

On the way there, Frank filled me in on the parents. Vincent Lux worked for a successful merchant and Erdwyn Lux helped run a stall in the market. They had been married for over ten years before they had their child, but not for lack of trying; Conception rates with long-lived species are fairly low. In fact, it wasn't uncommon for human-elf couples to never have children. That just goes to show how dire the situation is if there are more half-elves than elves in the world.

"Please, tell me everything that happened," I implored the couple.

Mr. Lux nodded, "All right. It was about an hour ago when I came home to find strange men in our home. They had one hand on my wife and were trying to take her, but she struggled fiercely. I didn't hesitate to jump in and pull the man away from her."

I looked at the wife and noticed she had slight bruising on her wrist, and the man himself was a little battered.

"After a moment, one of them shouted at the other to forget her and leave. They grabbed a large sack they had with them and ran out the door. It wasn't until Erdwyn screamed that they had Aeif that I understood what was in it."

The man clenched his fists so tight his knuckles went white, and the woman started shaking and sobbing harder as they recounted the events.

"If only I hadn't let them go..." Vincent Lux began to mumble.

"If you had tried to stop them from leaving, it's possible you would be dead. Then they would have taken your wife as well, and who knows how long it would have been until we arrived."

"B-But I-"

"Vincent, focus." I interrupted.

He took a deep breath and looked me in the eye, determination resounding from within.

"I need you to tell me what these men looked like," I asked with a gentle but affirming tone.

"I understand but, I didn't get a good look at their faces."

"Anything about them could help."

Mr. Lux nodded and proceeded to describe the men as well as he could remember. There were three men, one of them had a lumbering figure while the other two were skinny. They each wore dark clothing and masks, and the larger one never spoke. One of the skinny men was left-handed and seemed like the leader. The left-handed one had a short sword, the other skinny one held daggers, and the large one had a curved blade that Mr. Lux described as "Evil looking".

"I'm sorry I couldn't be of more help," Mr. Lux looked down in dejection.

"No, you've been quite helpful," I reassured him.

I stood from my seat and began to turn to the investigators when I felt a tug at my coat. Mrs. Lux, who had been quiet until now, had leaped from the couch and was now holding onto my coat and staring up at me, tears streaming from her eyes.

"P-Please, you have to find him! You have to find my baby!" Her statement was filled with stuttering and sniffling and such deep despair that it shook the very foundation of my soul.

I looked the crying mother in the eyes, "I will find him. I promise you; I won't stop until he's brought home."

The force of my words startled even me for a moment. I had never spoken with such determination and reassurance before. The power of a grieving mother is not one to take lightly.

She let go of me as her husband pulled her back to the

couch and she buried her head in his chest, though her tears had lessened some.

I turned back to the slightly shaken investigators and motioned for us to speak outside.

"That was impressive, though I will say that making that promise wasn't a good move."

As soon as we made it outside, Frank began to speak with me.

"Why is that?"

"The first rule of being an investigator is to never make a promise you can't keep."

I understood the idea behind this. If I promised I would find their son, then if I failed they would blame me. The guilt of such a situation had probably ruined many investigators.

"That's a good rule, but you're forgetting something," I retorted, "I'm not an investigator, and I have no intention of failing."

Frank put his hand to his forehead and shook his head.

"Well, I was impressed by your display," Khris said.

"I never said it wasn't impressive, I just didn't want Elric to make a promise he couldn't keep," Frank sighed, "But you seem determined enough, so I guess we should move on. What did you think of the situation?"

I pondered the information we had gathered for a moment before responding.

"I have to agree with you, it feels like targeted kidnapping."

"Damn, I had hoped we were wrong."

"Tsk, I don't know if I should feel disappointed or happy that we were right."

Right after Khris's comment, he looked up with furrowed brows.

"Wait a second, I just thought of something."

"What?" Frank and I replied in unison.

"Well, if three armed men were trying to kidnap the kid and his mom, then why did they leave after the father showed up? There were three of them versus one unarmed guy."

Oh... I hadn't thought of it before, but now that Khris pointed it out the situation was a little strange.

"Do you think Vincent Lux was in on it?" Frank asked the question I had just come to.

"I'm not sure, that's why I asked."

The two investigators gave me a questioning look.

"I must admit it hadn't crossed my mind, but since we don't have any evidence to back up that theory I'm going to have to go with a different one. Maybe Mr. Lux putting up a fight was causing a ruckus and they were going to be discovered?"

Frank nodded with a thoughtful look on his face, "Indeed, that is a possibility. Though I wonder if it could be that the men only brought the weapons to intimidate people and were reluctant to kill anyone."

"Well, if you put it that way," Khris started, "It makes me think that maybe the father was left alive for a reason. Perhaps for ransom, but then that wouldn't fit the other kidnapping. This may be unrelated to the others."

I shook my head, "It's too much of a coincidence for me to be convinced of that."

"I feel the same," Frank agreed.

"I don't believe it either, but I felt the need to propose the possibility."

"So our working theory is that they either didn't want to kill Mr. Lux or they couldn't kill him, yes?"

"I would say so."

"Yes, that sounds about right."

"So we're on the same page then, good. By the way, when are the others supposed to be back?"

"They should return fairly soon."

"Good. Then while we wait, I would like to discuss what you think these kidnappers are doing this for."

I had some ideas that were floating around in my head, but I wanted to hear what they were thinking. We went back and forth between trafficking, personal vendettas, and other dubious reasons. We eventually agreed that the most likely was either to sell them to nobles as trophies or to satisfy some other sick desires. I wasn't sure which one pissed me off more.

Just as we reached the end of the conversation, I heard two sets of footsteps coming from the street.

"Hey, you're back! Did you find anything?" Frank called out to who I assumed were the people he hired.

I turned to the people he was talking to and was greeted by another unexpected sight.

"Sorry, not much luck," said a man in plate armor with an open-faced helm and a large shield in his left hand, "We asked around and some people saw a few suspicious figures but it didn't lead anywhere."

Next to him was a timid-looking girl with shoulder-length hair and a staff topped with a red crystal.

"S-Sorry we c-couldn't um... find them..."

I couldn't help but express my surprise.

"Woah. Reginald, and Myrril? Today's been full of unexpected reunions."

It was indeed the two people I met in the forest shortly after my escape from the Vale.

"Oh hey, it's Elric. What are you doing here?" Reginald looked just as surprised as I was.

"E-Elric?" Myrril gasped.

"Oh? You all know each other?" Frank asked curiously.

I nodded, "Yeah, I met these two when I got lost in the forest outside town."

"That's a bit of an understatement don't you think?" Reginald jumped in, "You scared us nearly half to death when you chased that direwolf our way."

"To be fair, I didn't know anyone was there."

I really didn't, I swear!

"Woah, you were hunting a direwolf!?" Khris asked in astonishment.

"I-It was b-big..." Myrril mumbled.

It wasn't actually very large for a direwolf, I'd seen bigger outside Tors, but I wasn't going to say it.

"Yeah, I would show you but I already sent it to the butcher."

One of the first days I arrived I found a decently-priced butcher and decided to donate the meat to them but asked for the hide.

"Wait! We're getting sidetracked here," Frank interjected, "You can catch up later but for now, we need to find a missing child."

An Unexpected Mission

"You're right, this is much more important," I was a little embarrassed that I almost got caught up in chatting.

"Now that we're all together, let's head back inside. The family of the missing kid has lent us their table."

Everyone nodded and followed Frank into the house. I was in awe at their professionalism at work; the ability to change gears so quickly was impressive.

Frank and Khris led us into a little side room where a small table sat surrounded by four chairs. On the table was a smattering of rolled-up parchment surrounding a map of the city being held open by a candlestick and a few cups placed in the corners.

"Frank and I set this up earlier in case we needed it, and I would say we need it," Khris explained.

"I concur. Without anything concrete on the whereabouts of the kidnappers, we'll need to piece together what evidence we have and come up with something," Frank nodded along.

"Then let's start by sharing what we know."

We all gathered around the table and began laying out everything we knew about the kidnapping. Frank and I started with a recap of what's been going on before Reginald took over.

"We questioned some people in the area and a few said they witnessed three men with a large sack heading down this road in a hurry," He pointed to a street on the map not far from where we were.

"They said it was three men?" I asked.

He nodded in response.

"Then we can only assume it was the same three we are looking for. What happened next?"

"Well, we followed the trail of witnesses until we met a dead end. Literally." His finger moved to a section of the map a little ways away from the first place he mentioned, "This map isn't perfect so it's not on here, but there is an alley here that ends in a brick wall."

"And the three men were seen entering this alley?"

"Yes," Reginald replied, "The alley was completely devoid of doors or windows. It was just one of the many quirks of the city."

"Hmm."

I studied the map and the area around where Reginald pointed, but it didn't show anything that jumped out at me.

I turned to Frank, "Can you mark where the other kidnappings took place?"

"I can, but I don't know the exact locations," he replied with a raised eyebrow.

"That's all right, as long as it's within the same general area."

"I'm not sure where this is going," Khris muttered as Frank began to place markers all over the map. It had to total over a hundred by the time he finished.

"I think that's all of them."

"Thank you, this will be a great help."

I looked over the map once more, now with markers placing the last known locations of the many missing people. It only took me a moment to find something odd.

"Frank," I asked, "Are you sure this is all of them?"

"Huh? Well, there might be one or two I forgot but this should be the majority. Why?"

Just as he finished asking, his eyes grew wide as they fixated on the map.

"It's just that, there aren't any reports of people missing from the farms just outside the city," I explained.

The markers Frank placed on the map were all clustered in the "towns" within the city, and not a single one was from the numerous farms outside the walls.

"Woah, you're right," Reginald exclaimed, "I know for sure there are half-elf farmers out there, I even personally know a few."

"That was going to be my next question."

"A-And what about um... t-the other s-side o-f the river..."

Myrril pointed towards the eastern side of the river, which had its own cluster of buildings and was about the same size as the others but it had very few markers.

I looked to Frank, "Are there fewer people of elven blood on that side?"

"I don't think so. I mean, I can't think of a reason for that to be the case."

"Hmm."

This led me to the second odd thing I noticed. It seemed that the further from the Inner District, the fewer markers there were.

"I think the kidnappers are based out of, or at least near, the Inner District. Look at how the markers are distributed." I showed the others what I was seeing.

"I just noticed that as well," Khris said.

"Well, that narrows it down a bit. It's not too easy to get property in the Inner District." Frank began, "It does seem a little too simple, but it's the best lead we have."

"True, something feels a little strange as well. Though I suppose it's better than nothing. This isn't as simple as the last case."

Something Khris said right then sent a tingle through the back of my skull, and I remembered something from when I first ran into them.

"Khris, you might be a genius!" I exclaimed.

Ignoring the confusion on his face, I turned to Reginald.

"Tell me everything you saw in that alley!"

"What?"

"Just do it."

Reginald, still confused, recounted everything he saw. It was a long alley with trash all over the floor, the ground was uneven so there were puddles, but the last thing he said was what I was looking for.

"... And there was a metal grate in the back of the alley."

"I knew it!"

Everyone else seemed lost as to why I was so excited, so I ended up having to explain.

"There is an old sewer system running under the Inner District, something that Khris pointed out when we first met. I was trying to figure out how the kidnappers disappeared from the alley and how they kept getting away without witnesses."

"That's a good theory, but there aren't any sewers in the rest of the city." Frank pointed out.

I shook my head, "I was reading up on the history of the city the other day and one of the chapters was about the expansion of the sewer system into the rest of the city. Now, it was never finished but the system was extended under this neighborhood."

"The kidnappers can't go too far from a sewer entrance. Hence why they are clustered so strange!"

After Frank's statement, everyone's eyes widened. It seemed that everyone understood what I was saying. Frank and Khris nodded at each other and turned to the group.

"We are going to follow this lead before it's too late. Reginald and Myrril, lead the way!"

CHAPTER 6

Husks

"I was right, it's an unfinished sewer extension."

We were all gathered in the alley that Reginald and Myrril led us to and were staring through the grate in the ground.

"Hey, Reginald. Help me with this, will you?"

I got into a squat and held one end of the grate while gesturing to him to come and help. Reginald understood right away and grabbed the opposite side. Together, we hefted the heavy iron grate from the ground and set it against the wall. I could have just lifted it myself, but a few days ago I decided to try and hide my true abilities and limit myself to feel more human.

"Alright... Who's going first?" Khris asked.

They each looked at each other reluctantly, so I shrugged and jumped right through the two-foot-wide hole and into the underground passage. I landed on a stone walkway about fifteen feet below.

"Huh. I've never known anyone to so readily jump into a sewer," Frank remarked from above.

One by one they followed after me, with Reginald helping Myrril down at the end.

"Okay, which way do we go?" Reginald asked.

I had been scanning the area from under the grate and found that the tunnel continued in two directions, however, I was certain of which way we needed to start looking.

"Well, we aren't going that way," I pointed behind me, "It's a dead end."

"What? How can you even see that far?" Reginald squinted down the pitch-black tunnel.

"Light."

A bright light shone from the head of Myrril staff.

Interesting, so this is a spell?

I watched as Megin from the air gathered into her staff as she spoke, causing the light to burst forth from her focus at the top. From that, I deduced that spells use Megin from the environment rather than from the caster to cause an effect.

"That works." Frank, who had been taking out a few torches, remarked.

Khris mumbled, "Man, I wish I knew how to do that."

It wasn't something too difficult to learn in the grand scheme of things. I knew how to do something similar using my own Megin but Myrril beat me to it.

Myrril pointed her light down the tunnel I had talked about, "E-Elric was r-right..."

Her light shone about fifty feet down the tunnel where it abruptly stopped at a rough stone wall. Besides the bits of stone and rocks on the ground and roots poking through the bare wall, the tunnel was completely empty.

So we ended up walking in the other direction. The tunnel itself was about eight feet at the highest point. It was about twenty feet wide with a sluice running between the seven-foot wide walkways to either side. With the curved ceiling, however, we ended up walking in a line.

"I'm surprised it doesn't smell bad down here," Reginald remarked.

"That's because it was never finished so the only thing that makes its way down here is storm runoff," I explained.

We continued down the slightly musty tunnel for a while, with Frank in the lead, Myrril and Reginald behind him, and Khris bringing up the rear. It only took us a few minutes before we ran into our first problem.

"So uh, it looks like an intersection up ahead," Frank called out.

Indeed, in front of us was a four-way intersection of sewer tunnels, each one was as dark as pitch and silent beyond the scurrying of rodents.

"Myrril, could you point that light down these tunnels?"

"Mhm," She replied.

She pointed her staff down each tunnel in sequence, revealing several smaller side tunnels and not much else.

"Well shit, it's a maze," Khris said with a tinge of frustration.

I began looking for any clues as to where the kidnappers had gone, but I was having trouble with the small area we could move in. All I could see was some dirt, and I really didn't want to step into the stagnant water running through the tunnels, even if it wasn't sewage.

"Anyone have any idea which way to go?" Frank asked.

"We could just pick one and go," Reginald said after a moment.

"We could also split up and check each tunnel," Khris added.

Myrril, who had gone white at the suggestion, shook her head in protest.

"P-Please d-don't leave me!"

"We won't make you go anywhere by yourself," Reginald reassured Myrril, "By the way, do you know any spells for tracking people?"

Myrril shook her head, "N-No, sorry..."

Reginald looked at me hopefully.

I shook my head, "I could do a few things, but I don't think it's necessary."

"Huh?"

I pointed at the ground, "I figured out how to find them, so magic is unnecessary."

They all looked down at what I was pointing at.

"I don't see anything."

"I-It's just d-dirt..."

"What do you mean?"

"Is there something we can't see?"

Each person said something about their lack of understanding. Funnily enough, Myrril got the closest.

"Myrril's right, it's dirt."

They all looked at me with confusion.

I couldn't help but sigh, "I didn't notice when we were near the grate because there was dirt everywhere, but now that we are farther from it I realized that it didn't make any sense."

"Ah, I get it. You think the kidnappers tracked it in on their boots."

"I do," I responded, "There is a small trail of brown dirt running through the dust and bits of stone on the ground. I bet that if we follow this, it will lead us to them."

"Are you sure it wasn't just us that brought it in?" Reginald asked

"Let's find out. Myrril, could you follow the trial with your light?"

She nodded and began to move her staff over the dirt, shining light on the trail of dirt. It ran past all of us and turned right at the intersection.

"Nice find Elric," Frank slapped me on the back with a light chuckle and started down the tunnel, lighting a torch as he went.

We followed behind him and continued down the tunnel, which eventually took a light bend to the left and into another intersection. The trail of dirt wound through the labyrinthine tunnels in a confusing and calculated way. It felt as if the kidnappers expected to be followed and took this path specifically to lose anyone on their tail.

The dirt trail eventually ended, but we picked up footprints in the dust and followed them even further into the unfinished tunnels. We couldn't tell the time down there, but I figured it had been about half an hour since we first entered.

We were walking down another path past old blankets and other discarded cloth sitting in the stagnant water when Reginald spoke up.

"Hey, Elric."

"Yeah?"

"You said this place wasn't finished, right?"

"Huh? Yeah, it was never fully connected to the rest of the system, why?"

"Well, if it was never connected then what is all this trash doing in the water?"

"Um, maybe they fell through a grate?"

"But there aren't any grates here and the water is stagnant. Now that I think about it, it also smells a little funny."

It took Reginald to point it out for me to realize, but the air had started to smell a little rotten. The piles of random cloth in the water had also started to bother me since Reginald said something.

I focused a little more on the trash in the water and a very faint glow came from the large clumps. It was Megin.

Just then, one of the clumps jittered and started to move.

"They're alive!" I shouted to the rest of the group as I drew my blade.

The other mounds began to move and emit an air of hostility. They began to rise from the ground and revealed a horrifying sight. They were not mounds of trash, but some kind of humanoid creatures.

They had grey skin that reeked of death and pink pustules that covered their body. Their heads were covered in strange flesh bulbs, and long claws emerged from their fingertips.

We were surrounded.

"What the hell are these!?" Frank shouted.

"I have no idea, but they don't seem friendly," I shouted back.

I studied them as they just stood there staring at us. Some of them had bulbs that covered their whole head while overs had half their face exposed. The few eyes that were exposed were glossy, yet full of hatred.

They gave me pause as my heart began to race and my hands shook. They looked too close to *them*. It was a time of my life I did not wish to relive, much less remember.

I took a deep breath and forced the thought from my mind. They weren't the same, these were much different.

It was at that moment a shrill sound rang through the passage and caused me and my companions to wince in pain. The creatures had lurched back and shrieked; Their face bulbs undulating as the terrible sound emanated from them.

As quickly as it had started, the sound stopped. It was replaced by the splashing of water as all the creatures broke into a run straight for us.

Frank thrust his torch into the first creature's face, and the searing of meat echoed through the tunnel.

Khris followed after with a thrust from his rapier, finishing the creature off. Frank tossed his torch down and began defending himself. It was obvious that they were used to fighting together, one defending while the other attacked, switching off to never let themselves get surrounded.

Shhhiiiing!

The sound of scraping metal resounded from the shield that Reginald thrust in front of a creature trying to attack Myrril. He swung his sword from behind the shield and it dug into the creature's body.

"Fire arrow!"

The light from Myrril's staff went out as a bolt of flame shot from the top of her staff and impacted the creature's head. It shrieked in pain as the fire began to engulf its bulb of flesh. Reginald quickly put it out of its misery with a thrust through the chest.

Three of them rushed at me, barely giving me time to see the others fight. I narrowly dodged the first strike, then realized I couldn't fight properly on this small walkway and leaped past the second creature, into the water.

It struck out at me and scraped my chest plate, which got it a kick in the head in return. I landed on my feet and swung my blade at the third creature, which put up an arm to block. At least, that's what I thought it was doing.

My blade dug into the arm and stopped in the bone. That's when I realized that these creatures had some intelligence in them. It sacrificed one of its arms to immobilize my blade.

As if to confirm this, the creature's other arm swung around and slashed at my back. Luckily, I raised my arm in time to grab the creature's wrist and prevent the strike, but I knew that the next time may not be the same.

"These things are smart, watch out!" I yelled at the others as I pulled my blade free.

From the corner of my eye, I saw Reginald go to block a strike, before pulling back and opting to dodge after hearing what I said. The creature he was fighting was about to use the blind spot of the shield to strike at Reginald's side, but he caught it thanks to my warning.

A few more bolts of flame flew down the hall, lighting up the area and setting several creatures on fire. I struck at the creature that sacrificed its arm and my blade easily dug into its side, too easily in my opinion considering I was limiting my strength.

I was constantly being attacked from all around me, but soon Reginald appeared to cover my back while Myrril continued to assist both groups with long-range attacks.

I removed the head from one of the creatures and moved to block an attack from a second when a third appeared from nowhere and brought its claws down upon me. Without thinking, I moved my arm to take the hit with my vambrace, and the claws tore through the metal and dug into my flesh below.

I yelped as a dull heat enveloped my forearm.

"You all right?" Reginald asked as he struck out at the creature.

"I'll be fine," I told him, "But we need to take out these things before they get a lucky shot in."

"Agreed!"

We continued to combat the creatures as the water under us turned red and fatigue began to kick in.

"*Fire Storm!*"

Just as we began to take hits, a wall of flame shot through the tunnel, and the death throes of the creatures filled the air. Myrril stood behind us, sweating profusely, as a dull light dissipated from her staff.

"Thanks for the save Myrril," I said, "It was starting to look rough."

"What about the investigators?" Frank interjected.

I looked over just in time to see the last creature falling to the ground as a rapier was pulled from its head.

"You guys okay over there?" Khris called out to us.

"Yeah, just some minor scrapes over here," I replied.

I sat on the side of the waterway and began to remove my vambrace. Bits of the metal had been pushed into my arm, causing the throbbing pain to spike as it was removed. My forearm was soaked in blood, but the bleeding itself had just about stopped.

"That doesn't look like a minor injury," Khris said as he walked over and saw the blood.

"It's not as bad as it looks."

I pulled a waterskin from my pocket dimension, which

elicited looks of surprise from both Kris and Frank, and began to wash the wound. The cuts had gone pretty deep, a wound that would require stitches if I were human.

I dried the area around the wound and tightly wrapped it in bandages. The pressure alleviated the pain somewhat, enough for me to continue forward.

"We should get you to a healer, that wound is deep," Frank said.

I shook my head, "I'll be fine, the missing kid is more important right now."

Frank had a stern look on his face, "I'm serious. You need healing magic or at least stitches."

I tried to tell Frank that I was fine, but he wasn't hearing it. He wanted me to head to a healer at that very moment.

"Okay fine, I'll get this taken care of," I relented, "But only after we save the kid, deal?"

He sighed, "Fine, but don't go doing anything to agitate that wound."

"Good," I got to my feet. "Now, did you guys figure out what these things are?"

While Frank and I were arguing, the others had been investigating the strange creatures, trying to figure out what they were and where they came from.

"We have an idea, but you're not going to like it," Khris replied.

"W-We think they're um... c-creatures called Husks..." Myrril explained, "T-They are the r-result of failed of, um..."

She looked to me for help but I had no idea what she was talking about, so there was nothing I could do.

"I-It's failed necromancy! The stronger the Megin the

bigger the mutations!" She finally managed to push out with a shout.

"Necromancy? I don't think I understand."

The term "Necromancy" was a new concept to me. It seemed that I would be learning even more new things.

As Myrril tried to get out the words, Reginald stepped in.

"You don't know what necromancy is? It's magic designed to manipulate the dead."

"Hold up, what!?"

The idea of defiling the dead with magic was beyond my comprehension. It seemed that in the millennium that had passed, humans invented a way to artificially create undead. I felt sick at the thought.

Then, another thought crossed my mind. *If these were undead, then who were they originally? Don't tell me...*

I ran to the body of one of the creatures that still had some facial features and confirmed my suspicions. I let out a few choice words in my native tongue that would have put a sailor to shame.

"Woah, what's all the shouting for?"

I turned to Khris, who had presented the question, and informed him of my discovery.

"These creatures used to be half-elf!" I gestured to the slightly pointed ear as I shouted.

The color drained from the faces of my companions; they all knew what it meant. The creatures, Husks as Myrril called them, were the missing people.

CHAPTER 7

The Mad Scientist

An underground laboratory – somewhere in Edren.

The dank stone room was filled with the sound of whirring and humming emanating from various strange devices around the room. Each one was made of brass or bronze and had bright red crystals affixed in varying places. Tubes passed from one machine to the other and all around the floor, converging at a wooden table in the back.

A figure was hunched over a table covered in papers and test tubes, mercilessly writing away with a quill. The scratching of pen on paper was paused only for moments at a time to reapply ink to the quill.

With a loud creak, the heavy metal door to the chamber opened. Three people holding a sack entered. They each wore black clothing and cloth face coverings, making it impossible to know their identities.

The figure at the table paused his writing and turned his head towards the door. An older, raspy voice came from his mouth with a light accent.

"I assume your interruption means you've brought me the new subjects."

His haughty attitude rubbed the three people the wrong way, but they knew better than to get on his bad side.

The one in the center, the larger one, dropped the sack they were holding. Next to him, the one with the sword on his hip spoke up.

"We were only able to get the kid, there was too much heat once the husband got there."

The man at the table took a deep breath, before hurling his inkwell at the one who spoke, which was easily dodged.

"You incompetent fools!" He spat, "I needed the elf more than the half-blooded trash!"

The one who spoke before responded, "There was too much noise, the guards had been called. There was no way for us to-"

"That's not my problem!" The man cut them off, yelling. "You should have just killed the husband and taken the elf!"

"Like I said, it wasn't possib-"

"Begone! I am done speaking to fools like you! I'll just have to make it work with the tainted child."

The man's voice was filled with superiority and confidence in his abilities.

"As you wish," The masked figure stated, "Would you like us to put him in one of the cages?"

"Hm? No, no, put him over there. My cages are currently... occupied," The man gave a hearty chuckle as the lumbering person moved the now-wiggling bag to the back of the room.

The one who seemed like the leader of the three bowed to the man, "Then we shall take our leave."

The man he was addressing paid him no mind as he started fiddling with various contraptions around the room, preparing for whatever experiment he was doing.

After being ignored the three cloaked figures left the room, closing the heavy steel door behind them.

"Gods, where do these things come from?"

Frank shouted as he defended against another Husk. We had continued following the trail and ended up fighting even more Husks on the way. Including the first group, we had to have taken out around thirty by then.

"Ugh... The smell..." Myrril was holding her nose while firing off spells.

Oh yeah, I forgot to mention that we had ended up following the tracks through a roughly dug passage and had ended up in the sewer proper. Needless to say, the smell was overwhelmingly bad.

The rank smell of refuse and rot was assaulting my senses, which made it difficult to pay attention to the enemies in front of us when we first entered, but I had since gotten used to it enough that it didn't affect my combat effectiveness.

"Hya!" I pulled my blade free from the last Husk in view and searched for more enemies. We were all on edge from being attacked over and over, but the bright side was that we were able to rest once in a while.

"See any more?" I asked the others.

"Nothing, I think we got them all in this area."

We let out a collective sigh of relief and relaxed a little bit.

"This is getting rough," Frank remarked.

Reginald nodded, "We should probably get out of here and tell the association. No offense, but I don't think the city guard is equipped for fighting these things."

"None taken," Franked waved off the statement, "I actually agree with you. The guard would probably take heavy losses. Times like these are when you call in professionals."

The others voiced their agreement, but I was reluctant to leave so easily. I felt the need to point out our original mission.

"I don't agree with leaving," I said with concern, "If we don't push forward, what will happen to Aeif?"

The others looked troubled once I mentioned the kid we had come to save.

"Elric... I don't want to be like this," Khris started," But, what if it's already too late?"

"And what if it isn't?" I snapped back, "Will we really doom that kid to die?"

Frank put a hand on my shoulder.

"Elric, calm down. I get what you're saying, but we'll have a better chance at saving him if we get help."

I looked him in the eyes, which were full of pain, and understood that he was just as broken up about this as I was. However, the anger in my heart and the desire to help the elves were too strong to agree with them.

I pulled away and turned my back to him.

"If you want to leave and get reinforcements, then be my guest. But I'm going to save him and there's nothing you can do to stop me."

My determination burned brighter as I made my decision. I needed to save Aeif. I knew the feeling of being alone in a strange place, helpless to do anything as certain death towered over you.

I refused to judge all humans as the same, but I couldn't help but wonder if the outcome would have been different if the kid was human.

When I finished my statement, I began to walk down the tunnel. I didn't quite know where I was going, but my gut was telling me to head that way.

Then, I heard footsteps behind me.

"Elric, wait up!"

It was Reginald.

"I told you, nothing you say will stop me."

"We're not trying to stop you," He said, "We're coming with you."

I stopped and turned to see Reginald and Myrril approaching from behind.

"You spoke the truth. It's our job to save this kid, and leaving now would be the same as failing."

It was Frank who spoke, he was following as well.

Khris approached as well and stood before me, scratching his head.

"Huh, you sure do know how to guilt trip someone."

I couldn't help but smile as Khris continued.

"I still think we should send some kind of message, but you're right about saving Aeif. I don't know how I would face his parents if..."

We all saw his parents and how much sorrow they must have felt, not knowing if they would ever see their son again. None of us wanted them to feel that for the rest of their lives.

I know how it feels to lose those you love, my entire family...

Emotion welled in my chest so I quickly pushed those thoughts from my mind. One day I would have to face it, but for now, it was best to bottle it up. To lose my composure in this situation would be a deadly mistake.

I happily looked at everyone, their expressions were much different from before. The look of reluctance had been replaced with a fire in their hearts.

Badum, Badum, Badum.

My eyes widened as I turned my head toward the sound. Time seemed to have slowed as a lumbering shape appeared from the darkened tunnel, speeding right toward us.

"Khris watch out!"

I shouted as I pushed Khris away from where he was standing. I turned to the shape and crossed my arms in front of me to block the charge. None of us had seen what it was yet, and I was the only one able to react in time.

"Guh!" The wind was knocked out of me as I was hit head-on, unable to block whatever it was. My arms were flung open and my chest was hit with what felt like a catapult. I felt air rush past me before my back connected with a hard surface that instantly cracked, sending stone raining over me, and the world went black.

Reginald was unable to comprehend what he had just seen. One moment Elric was smiling, then the next moment Khris was on the ground and Elric had been flung into the wall of the sewer. A cloud of dust had kicked up around him, but the sound of falling stones could be heard by all of them.

Heavy, animalistic breathing was coming from a hulking form standing just in front of where Elric landed.

Surprisingly, Myrril was the first to shake off her shock and pointed her staff toward the form. She quickly cast her light spell on the head of the staff and illuminated the tunnel.

There, facing away from them, was the massive back of a creature. It had grey skin with pink pustules dotted across it, much like the Husks. Its body was malformed. One leg was as thick as a tree while the other was as frail as a twig and was too short to reach the ground. The creature's back was arched as it hunched in the tunnel, meaning it was probably ten feet tall standing straight.

Its massive shoulders led to arms bigger than even his leg with fists akin to boulders, and fingers as thick as Reginald's arms.

GGGRRRROOOH

It let out a growl as it slowly turned its way toward the light, revealing its ugly and deformed face. Its massive shoulders grew larger than its head, making it look sunken into the creature's chest. Where its left eye should have been was instead a swollen pink growth that squirmed and fidgeted in the light. Its jaw was unhinged and the cheeks were ripped in such a way that the creature appeared to smile. Its only exposed ear, on the right side of its head, came to a sharp point.

"What the Fu-"

Frank was cut off as the creature opened its jaw, farther than any man or elf should be able to, and let out a deafening roar as its lengthy tongue flicked back and forth.

A massive fist swung towards Frank but was met with a

metal shield as Reginald jumped in front of him. The force of the impact pushed him back a few inches, but he was able to hold his shield steady.

"Where the hell did this thing come from!?" Reginald frantically shouted.

"I don't know, but it's definitely hostile!" Khris shouted from behind the beast as he plunged his rapier into its back again and again.

The creature swung his fist behind him, which Khris was just barely able to dodge. Then, Myrril's light went out and fire arrows began to appear in the air, hurling toward the creature. The only light they had was a torch on the ground and the occasional flashes caused by Myrril's magic.

"What about Elric?" Frank asked as he bolted from behind Reginald and struck the creature several times before retreating from another fist.

"I-I d-don't know!" Myrril shouted.

They all knew that he was probably dead; an impact like that surely crushed his chest. But they didn't want to say it, they wanted to hold on to hope that he was still alive.

"Myrril!" Reginald shouted, "Try something with more power! The fire arrows aren't doing much!"

He was right, Myrril's spells had been barely singing the creature's skin. She would need more firepower to do any real damage.

Myrril nodded, "*Fire Storm!*"

A whirlwind of fire kicked up around the beast, eliciting a horrifying roar as it was engulfed in flame. The others jumped back from the beast as its fists began flying through the fire. The spell ended a moment later and revealed the creature that was trapped within.

Its skin was badly burned and the bulb of flesh on its face had exploded, exposing a blackened skull, but it was still alive.

"Shit!" Reginald cursed, "It wasn't enough."

"How the hell is this thing still al- AAAUUGH!!"

Khris was cut off by a massive fist plowing into him and sending him flying across the chamber.

"Khris!"

My head hurts...

I slowly came to consciousness as pain racked my entire body. I felt like I had broken at least four ribs, and fractured a lot of other bones.

What was I doing again? I hear something, but what is it?

I opened my eyes and found I was buried under chunks of rock and stone. I had blood running down my face. I tried to move my arms and felt a sharp pain in my shoulder.

Must be dislocated; that's fine.

It wasn't the first time and wouldn't be the last time I had dislocated my arm. I slowly pulled myself out of the rubble and to my feet. My sight was still a little hazy, but I could clearly see something happening a little way down the tunnel. There were flashes of light and people shouting.

My eyes moved down to my chest, which still felt heavy. There, I saw my chest plate had crumpled inward. It wasn't puncturing my chest, so I wasn't too bothered.

What happened?

I wracked my foggy mind, and it hit me. My eyes focused forward as I remembered what happened. I saw a massive beast in the tunnel that looked similar to a gorilla, if said gorilla had one tiny leg, the head of a person, and no hair.

Fighting the creature was Reginald, holding a slightly dented shield; Myrril, who was internally and externally panicking; and Frank, who was using Reginald as cover. Off to the side was Khris, slumped against a wall and covered in blood.

I knew then that the monstrosity had been what hit me. I grabbed my dislocated arm and wrenched it back into place. The sharp pain increased tenfold as it spiked through my shoulder and made my legs weaken for a moment. I locked my eyes on the creature and studied its every movement.

"Myrril, you still good?" I heard Reginald shout.

"I-I'm still good to go!" The nervous Myrril responded.

"We need to change tactics, this isn't working!" Frank said as he stabbed at the creature.

Grasping my weapon, I got into my stance and took a deep breath. My bones creaked and my joints ached, but I pushed through it. I drew my blade and kicked off the ground, charging for the beast.

It didn't even see me as I leaped and stabbed by blade into his back, all the way to the hilt. The beast howled in pain as I dragged my blade down his back. It flung me off but I quickly recovered and used the wall as a foothold to push off and attack again.

The creature swung its massive arm toward me but it had lost a lot of control after I cut the muscles in its back, making dodging it child's play.

"Elric!?" Reginald shouted in surprise, "Man, am I glad to see you!"

I kicked off the creature and pulled my blade from its chest as it struck out at me, and landed next to Reginald.

"It may be undead, but its anatomy is the same," I explained, "Go for the tendons in its arms and legs."

I leaped for again, dodging another fist and an attempted kick. Though I admit that I didn't even need to dodge the kick since it tried to use its small leg for some reason.

My blade bit into its calf as I slid underneath it and jumped to my feet. Its arms began to swing wildly, damaging the stone holding the tunnel together. If left to its own devices, the creature may have brought down the tunnel and killed us all.

As one fist swung at Reginald, I saw him bring his blade down on the creature's wrist and its fist went limp. It brought its arm back and looked confused as to why it couldn't move its fingers.

I took this chance to rush its back once more and dig my blade into its other shoulder. It shook wildly as I was almost thrown off, but I managed to stay put and plant my legs on its back. With the sound of tearing flesh and rending bone, I used my body weight to drag the blade down its back at an angle and ripped through the spine on my way down.

It let out an earth-shaking roar as it collapsed to the ground. With it unable to move its lower body and its arms severely damaged, it was hardly a threat anymore; But we didn't let the opportunity go to waste. Frank, Reginald, and I all plunged our weapons through the creature's head and back until it stopped moving.

There was a moment of silence, where all that could be heard was heavy breathing and the slight movement of water.

"I'm not sure how you survived, but by the Gods am I glad you did," Frank said after a moment, his breathing ragged.

"It was a lot of luck," I said, trying to catch my breath.

"K-Khris!" Myrril yelled with urgency.

I looked over to see her knelt next to him, trying to stop the blood pouring from many wounds.

"Oh shit, Khris!" Panic filled Frank's voice as he ran to his partner. Reginald and I followed behind as we began to pull various bandages and healing salves from our coat and bag, respectively.

"I know some battlefield medicine," I stated, "It's just the basics, but it will help."

"Same here, I learned a bit of first aid," Reginald added.

We moved the other two aside and started to inspect Khris. He definitely had broken ribs and what sounded like a pierced lung. One of his arms was bent at an unnatural angle and he was moving in and out of consciousness.

"Did... we win?" He asked weakly.

"We did, Khris. We did," Frank started, "But you were hurt, so we're trying to help you."

"Oh... okay..." Khris's eyes began to close, "I'll just... take a nap then..."

"No, no! We can't have you going to sleep, all right? We need you to stay awake." Panic filled Frank's voice.

"My head..."

"It'll be okay, you just need to stay awake."

During that time, Reginald and I began to bandage as

many wounds as we could and apply a salve to the worst of them. A healing salve was a combination of medicinal and magical plants that worked to seal wounds and help heal them. It was nothing but a stop-gap measure, but they gave us enough time to get him to a doctor.

"He's lost a lot of blood, but I don't think it's life-threatening," I told Frank," But we should still get him out of here."

"El...ric?" Khris called out.

"Yeah, it's me," I replied while bandaging his head.

"Good... you're alive..."

"And you will be too," I said, "You probably have a bad concussion, so try to stay awake, okay?"

I turned to Frank, "We need to make a splint for his arm."

"I don't have anything that could help."

"Your scabbard," Reginald explained, "If we use yours and Khris's scabbards, we can probably make a good enough splint."

"Good thinking."

Frank didn't waste any time removing his scabbard and giving it to Reginald. Within a few moments, we had a serviceable splint. Now all we had to do was set his arm.

"Alright, Khris. This is going to hurt... a lot." I warned him, for which I got a nod in return.

I looked at Reginald and silently told him to do it. He grabbed Khris's arm and realigned the bone as quickly as he could. Khris let out a pained howl before losing consciousness.

"Khris!" Frank's voice was filled with despair.

"It's okay, he's still alive," I reassured him, "The shock made him lose consciousness."

"I'm all done over here," Reginald said, tying off the splint.

"Same," I nodded.

Frank was looking pale, but it was to be expected. His partner was in a rough spot.

"Now we just need to get him out of here," I mused.

"I got this," Frank walked over and carefully lifted his partner from the ground, "You guys need to go on ahead. I'll get him to a clinic and rejoin you as soon as I can."

"All right," I agreed, "There was a grate a little ways back,"

I gave Frank directions to the nearest sewer grate I had seen. He waved at us and promised once more to be back before carrying his wounded comrade down the tunnel.

"I-I hope Khris will... will b-be okay..." Myrril mumbled.

"I'm sure he'll be fine," Reginald said, "Right now I'm more worried about us."

"Y-you are?" Myrril asked.

"Yeah. I mean, we have no idea where we're going or if we'll run into another one of those things."

The trail we had followed to this point had vanished, but I had another idea about finding our way.

"It's pretty simple," I said, "If we see more Husks, that means we're going the right way."

Reginald looked dumbfounded. Not in the normal sense, more like he thought what I said was really stupid. The next words from his mouth confirmed this.

"Are you stupid! We nearly died fighting that thing and you want to go looking for them!?"

"Yep," I replied, "We know now that it doesn't use magic

to move, so damaging its musculature is the best way to defeat it."

Reginald let out a long, drawn-out sigh. It was the sigh of someone trying to cope with an unbelievable situation.

"B-By the way," Myrril started, "um... what was t-that thing? I-It was bigger and s-stronger than the others..."

"Yeah, I was thinking about that too," Reginald added, "Any ideas Elric?"

I nodded, "I think it was one of the missing elves."

If Myrril was right and these Husk's mutations depended on how much Megin the person had, then the big one must have had a lot of it. Since the smaller ones were half-elf, who have significantly less Megin than elves, it was only natural to assume the big one was once elven.

The others nodded along as I explained my thought process and reasoning.

"Hm, that makes sense to me," Reginald said.

Myrril nodded thoughtfully, "N-Now that I... um... think about it, I saw a p-pointed ear on its head."

"That just adds to my suspicions, "I said, "Though now I'm starting to wonder just how many elves went missing."

Frank had said the missing people were elven and half-elven, but he never specified how many of each. We knew there were just over a hundred missing people just from the marks Frank had placed on the map, but we had no idea how many were elves.

I figured that the only thing we could do was press onward and hope there weren't that many.

We quickly patched ourselves up and continued on our way. We had no time to waste and decided to pick up the pace. Of course, with increased pace comes increased noise.

Husks were quickly alerted to our arrival and literally jumped at the opportunity to catch us off guard. Unbeknownst to them, we had considered the consequences of our actions and were prepared for them.

"Reginald and Myrril, take the three on the left, I'll handle the two over here."

"Got it!"

"U-Understood!"

We were slowly becoming a coherent team. I would assess the situation and give orders to the others. Reginald instantly jumped in front of the enemy and stopped them with his shield, Myrril fired spells at them from the back, and I either took on the remaining enemies or I distracted them until the others could assist.

Shouts and screeches echoed through the sewers as we carved a path of carnage through the undead, following them back to their source.

After stopping for a moment to catch our breath, we noticed some strange sounds coming from a path up ahead. It was like the guttural sound of a sleeping beast.

We quietly made our way to the opening of the tunnel and I took a peek into the darkness. I saw several shapes a little way down the passage, one large one and what looked like five smaller ones.

"It's a group of six," I whispered, "One of them is a big guy."

"Why did a big one have to show up now?" Reginald

groaned in a hushed tone, "We haven't seen any this whole time so I was hoping the one we fought had been it."

"I-If only we were that l-lucky..." Myrril muttered.

I moved back to look down the tunnel, just to make sure we didn't miss anything when I saw what looked like a door just past the Husks.

"Guys, I think there's a door down there," I informed the others.

"Really?" Reginald took a peek, "It's pitch black, how the hell can you see anything?"

"Carrots, I ate a lot of carrots," I whispered sarcastically.

"I-I thought that was a myth..." Myrril trailed off.

It was obvious that the sarcasm went over her head, but I figured it would take too long to explain the joke in this situation.

Reginald rolled his eyes, "Fine, I guess it doesn't really matter. What matters is our plan."

"I have an idea," I turned to Myrril, "Can you still do that Fire Storm?"

Myrril nodded, "I-I can..."

"Good, then we'll start with that," I continued, "Myrril's spell should take out the small Husks. Then, Reginald and I will rush the big Husk."

"That sounds good, but how exactly should we go about killing that monstrosity?" Reginald interrupted.

"Good question," I said, "Since we already know they don't move with magic like normal undead, we can take advantage of their anatomy. Even if a single strike to the head or heart won't take it down, all we have to do is sever its spine and cut its tendons."

"Speaking of which, I meant to ask you something,"

Reginald began, "You had cut the spine of that direwolf when we first met, which is already insane, but now you're doing it again and suggesting I do it as well. What I'm trying to say is, how the hell are you slicing through bone that easily!?"

Reginald raised his voice slightly from the group whisper when asking that question. Honestly, I had wondered why the Husk's bones were so easily cut through, but I had attributed it to them being undead.

"I think it's partially because I'm aiming for the right spots, and partially because their bones are already rotted and brittle," I replied.

"I... I have nothing to say," Reginald sighed, "That makes complete sense."

"Good, then we're all on the same page?"

Both of them nodded in response.

"Myrril, on your go," I prompted.

She closed her eyes and began to concentrate. This time, I was able to watch closely as she prepared to cast her spell. Small glowing particles from the air, similar to dust, began floating toward her staff and gathering at the top. What had started as clear-colored energy rapidly changed to a fiery red.

Myrril opened her eyes and stepped into the opening of the tunnel, pointing her staff at the darkened space.

"*Fire Storm!*"

As she shouted the name, a burst of hot air filled the space as a whirlwind of fire burst from the bloodstone affixed to the top of the staff. The flames licked down the tunnel at an incredible pace and soon filled the space from wall to wall.

The screams of Husks burning alive once again echoed

through the tunnels and but a moment later, the Fire Storm had died down.

Reginald and I took that moment to dart around the corner and rush the large Husk, which was the only one still alive at that point. I could see just fine in the dark, but Reginald couldn't so Myrril quickly summoned light just as her other spell faded, illuminating the tunnel and giving us a clear view of our target.

"Change of plans," I shouted to Reginald as we ran, "I'm going to distract the Husk while you disable it."

"What!? Are you serious!?" Reginald yelled in disbelief.

"Yeah. I mean, look at that thing. It's perfect to practice precision strikes on. You did want to know how to cut through bone, didn't you?"

Reginald grumbled something under his breath before agreeing to my idea.

I turned back to look at the Husk. It had massive legs like an elephant, a thick torso, and tall shoulders. It also had the smallest, shriveled, necrosis-ridden arms I had ever seen. I honestly would have been laughing at the mummified-looking appendages if I hadn't known what the creature was.

The Husk turned to look at us after the fire had burned its back. It let out a terrifying roar from the pink bulb that covered where its head should have been and started to charge at us.

I rushed forward and slashed, giving it a deep gash in the stomach. The Husk tried to swipe at me but its arms wouldn't move, so it just looked like it was moving its shoulder in some strange dance.

"Kyah!" Reginald flanked behind it and struck its back with a wide slash. "Tsk, I only nicked the bone."

His cut had been both too shallow and in the wrong place.

"You shouldn't be aiming for the bone," I explained while jumping back from a massive foot heading at me, "You need to aim for the spots *between* the bones."

"Between?" Reginald shouted, "How the hell am I supposed to know where that is!?"

"Practice!" I replied.

Reginald gripped his blade and rushed back in, hitting the Husk again before backing off. We continued our dance for a few minutes before Reginald finally cut into the Husk's spine and it collapsed to the ground. I quickly followed up his attack by parting the downed creature's head from its shoulders.

Myrril ran up to Reginald, who was trying to catch his breath from all the exertion.

"Y-you did it!" she said cheerfully.

"Yeah... I did, didn't I?" he said before turning to me, "That's not as easy as you make it look."

I nodded, "I know. It took years of practice to learn and I wasn't even the best at it. I remember back in basic training when-"

I cut my reminiscing short when I realized I said more than I should have. I just hoped that they would ignore it.

"Basic training?" Reginald asked, "Are you a soldier?"

Reginald, why did you have to ask!?

I screamed internally at my luck as I responded to Reginald's question.

"Just, please forget what I said."

Reginald looked like he wanted to say something, but decided to drop it.

"U-Um," Myrril decided to speak up in the middle of this awkward situation, "D-Didn't you say there was a door?"

"Y-Yes!" I internally thanked Myrril for changing the subject, "I did see a door, it was over... there."

I pointed at what appeared to be a massive slab of metal embedded in the wall. It was fairly plain except for the large handle in the center.

"I have a feeling they were guarding this," I told the others.

I started to reach for the handle when Reginald stopped me.

"Woah, wait a second. We should come up with a plan to take whoever's in there by surprise."

"They probably already know we're here, we weren't exactly quiet," I retorted, "Though we should be ready to fight the moment we open the door."

I grasped the handle and looked back to make sure everyone was ready before giving it a tug.

The door was very heavy and let out a loud *Creeeaaaak* as I pulled it open. The foot-thick steel door gave way to a dimly lit chamber filled with all manner of strange devices. Each one was made of shiny bronze-like metal and had strange tubes leading out of them. Red crystals were affixed to every device, discharging a large amount of magical energy.

All of the tubes snaked across the ground and converged at the back of the room where a figure was standing with it's back to us, feverishly working on something in front of him.

We rushed into the room and took a defensive position in front of the door.

"Hey!" I shouted, "Turn around, nice and slow."

The figure froze and turned its head to look over its shoulder. A raspy, older voice began to speak.

"Who am I? Hehehehehe. WHO AM I?" The figure spun around to face us, spreading his arms out in a theatrical fashion.

"I am the great Koberic, the scientist who discovered the secret to immortality!" He shouted arrogantly.

But I didn't ask who he was...

"The real question that needs to be asked here," He continued, "Is who the hell are YOU! You scum of the earth who prance around, destroying my experiments, and invading my lab!"

I couldn't help but think, *"Is this guy for real?"* and I had a feeling the others were thinking the same.

"You do not understand the gravity of your crimes!" Koberic continued, "I am the greatest scientist that ever lived! To interrupt my most important research is-"

The rambling man on the other end of the room seemed to be a human in his sixties. He had a tall, oval face with crazy white hair, beady little eyes, and a massive smile that looked borderline psychotic.

"-will bring down the force of the world upon you! You will be crushed like the insects you are!"

Wow, he really likes the sound of his own voice.

"H-He must like the s-sound of his own voice..." Myrril whispered to me with comedic timing.

"Are you the one who's been kidnapping people?" Reginald asked, completely ignoring the man's rambling.

"I don't like the tone of your voice," Koberic squinted at him, "You should be bowing before me! Oh, but I cannot fault you for not understanding my goals with such a tiny insect brain," He pulled his hand to his face in a dramatic way, "But to answer your question, yes. I am the one acquiring test subjects from the undesirables in the city above me."

The way he spoke about the elves and half-elves rubbed me the wrong way. Just as I was about to say something, Koberic stepped to the side and revealed the table behind him.

Laying on the table was an unconscious child with slightly pointed ears. The tubes coming from all the machines were connected to various points on his body, and a grueling-looking blade sat next to him.

"This is unforgivable!" I shouted, nearly slipping into my native tongue.

"Oh?" Koberic responded, "You actually care for these filthy creatures? Then I suppose you'll have to be disposed of."

He pulled a lever on the wall, and several clanking sounds echoed in the chamber.

"It's a shame really, you could have witnessed a miracle." His mouth twisted in a wicked grin.

Out of nowhere, three of the big Husks blocked our path. One of them had tiny legs but massive arms and body, another had a very lithe torso, but huge arms and legs, and the third one had its entire body mutated except for one arm.

"Now then, let's get this experiment going, shall we?" Koberic picked up the blade from the table and began to hum a cheerful song.

Meanwhile, the Husks had started their attack. We were in an enclosed space, making it harder to fight, but I didn't care. My mind was on saving Aeif.

One of the Husks swung an arm at me, which I dodged while not even looking. I was pissed off by Koberic and I wasn't going to let him get his way.

"Sorry, I'm going to have to have you guys handle them," I said to my companions.

"Huh?" was all Reginald was able to say between dodging attacks.

I held my hand in the air and pulled an item from my pocket dimension. Appearing in my hand was a six-foot-long spear with intricate details carved into the head and shaft. It was one of the weapons I had received from my father after basic training, the second of three.

I hefted the spear up and aimed it through a gap in the wall the Husks had formed. Throwing it like a javelin, I threaded the spear through an opening and watched it fly through the air. A moment later, the sound of glass shattering could be heard as the spear pierced through one of the machines and embedded itself in the wall.

The smile on Koberic's face vanished, "NO! You don't understand what you have just done!"

His frustration was apparent and led me to believe I destroyed something important.

"I will make you feel a thousand deaths for this!" He raged, before looking down at the kid on the table, "And I'll start with him."

Koberic raised his blade high above Aeif with the intent to plunge it down, but I wasn't about to let him do it.

I drew my sword in a reverse grip and slid under the legs of the Husk in front of me. I slashed behind me as I jumped to my feet and heard a loud thump, like a large creature dropping to the ground.

My feet kicked off the ground and I accelerated across the room just in time to intercept Koberic's blade. An anguished howl filled the room and a wet thump sounded nearby.

I turned and pointed my weapon at Koberic, standing between him and Aeif. Koberic was crying out in pain and holding his forearm as blood gushed from where his hand had once been.

"You!" He shouted through gritted teeth, "I'll make you pay for taking the hand of my esteemed self!"

Even in mortal danger, he's still being arrogant.

Then, there was a slight tingle in the back of my head as I noticed small amounts of energy begin to gather around Koberic.

"I am the greatest mind in all of Talmara. You cannot possibly fight against the smartest man in the world! If you surrender now, I may forgi- GUURRRGHH!"

Blood poured from his mouth as my blade pierced his chest. The energy that was gathering had dissipated, and Koberic's arms fell limply to his sides.

As the light left his eyes, I whispered in his ear.

"Kyrtvale awaits."

I pulled my blade from his chest and his lifeless body slumped to the ground. I quickly spun around and checked on Aeif. I wanted to remove the tubes from his body, but I was unsure of how they were attached. For the moment, I knew he would be okay, so I turned my attention back to the Husks at the entrance.

Kyrtvale – Lord Atre's office.

"My lord!" A small creature rushed through the ornate doors at the entrance to the Overseer's office.

The man behind the bone-white desk sighed.

"**Grimwa, my treasured assistant. Give me a reason not to kill you this time.**"

The man behind the desk was Lord Atre, Overseer of Kyrtvale. His skin was a swirling storm of deep burgundy and cobalt blue. Horns protruded from his forehead and curled backward over his head. Feathers protruded from his wrist and behind his ears, and he had a scaled tail with a dagger-like point.

His assistant, Grimwa, was a tiny creature with a sharp face and impish features. He shook in his well-tailored suit as his master glared at him.

"B-But Master, it's good news!" Grimwa started, "The mad scientist you've been waiting for has finally arrived!"

"**Oh?**" A toothy grin spread across Lord Atre's face, "**This is indeed good news. How did he finally die?**"

Grimwa started to sweat, "Well, um... the thing is..."

He had hoped with all his might that Lord Atre wouldn't ask, but now he had to answer the question.

"He was killed by... an escapee." Grimwa braced himself to be slaughtered, disemboweled, and thrown from the highest tower. Instead, his Lord let out a hearty laugh.

"**It was the most recent one yes? He's done me a great service, so great I may be persuaded to forgive his transgressions.**"

Lord Atre was ecstatic. He had been waiting for the mad

scientist Koberic to die for many decades. He was a thorn in Atre's side that defiled the sanctity of life and death.

"**Grimwa.**"

"Y-Yes, my lord?"

"**Keep me informed of the escapee's movements. His actions amuse me.**"

"Um... Y-Yes Lord Atre!" Grimwa managed to say. He had never been asked anything like this before, so his confusion was understandable.

Atre stood from behind his desk and made his way to the doors.

"**If anything comes up, I'll be with our guest,**" He chuckled, "**He's been such a thorn in my side, I'll handle his initiation personally.**"

CHAPTER 8

Is this the end?

After I rejoined the fray, the battle ended fairly quickly. Reginald and Myrril had backed out of the still-open door and blocked the Husks from going after them with the shield. This left me open to attack them from behind. It only took a moment for me to rend their backs to ribbons, ending the threat.

"I'm not sure if I should be mad, or impressed," Reginald sighed.

I scratched the back of my head, "I'm sorry for leaving you hanging. If I hadn't acted the kid would be dead."

"I know," Reginald's voice had a tinge of anger, "But that doesn't change the fact that we could have died! There's no way we could have fought two of them at once. I mean, Myrril doesn't even know any close-range spells!"

"I'm truly sorry. I had faith you would have figured something out, and I didn't even know Myrril couldn't fight at close range." I tried to get my feeling across.

I really didn't know that Myrril couldn't fight at close range. It was only logical that mages have different options for different ranges, though I suppose my logic may be outdated.

"I-It's okay... it all w-worked out in the end, r-right?" Myrril stated.

Reginald gave another sigh, "I suppose you're right; it did work this time," He turned to me, "However, don't ever do that again, okay?"

"I understand," I responded.

"HEEEEEEEY!" Just then, a voice echoed through the tunnel. "ARE YOU GUYS OKAY!?"

I looked towards the source of the voice and saw Frank sprinting down the tunnel at high speed, torch in one hand while waving his other. Behind him were several other figures bearing torches.

One of them wore a similar uniform to Frank and Khris, a trench coat over hardened leather armor, and a longsword at their side. Then there were four guards in standard armor carrying short spears in their hands and blades on their waists. There were also a few other people with varying armor and weapons, probably more mercenaries from the Association, escorting a couple of men in white coats carrying cases.

"Yeah, we're okay," I replied as Frank and the others caught up to us.

"Good. I brought what backup I could muster on such short notice," He gestured behind him.

One of the men in the white coats approached me and began to open his case, "You're injured, we need to take care of it before the wound becomes infected."

"No, take care of the kid first," I pointed the doctor to the room, "He's attached to some kind of machine. I couldn't figure out how to safely remove him."

The doctor peeked into the room and his eyes went wide.

Speechless, he grabbed the other doctor and ran into the room, followed by the mercenaries.

"You found the kid!?" Frank asked, "How is he?"

"He's alive," I responded, "It was close, but we made it just in time."

Frank let out a sigh of relief.

"How about Khris," I asked, "Is he okay?"

"Yeah, he's doing good. The docs were able to fix his ribs with a bit of magic, but he'll still be needing bed rest for a while."

"By the way, who's your friend?" I nodded at the scene unfolding in front of us.

"Right, this is a crime scene," The man in the trench coat began instructing the guards. "Secure the site and report anything ye find out of the ordinary. Who knows what roams down 'ere, yeah?"

The guards gave a salute and began to carry out their orders.

"Oh, right. Elric, I want you to meet a co-worker of mine," Frank waved over the man in the trench coat.

"Elric, right?" The man stuck his hand out, "The name's Sean McCloud, it's a pleasure to meet ye."

"Same here," I shook his outstretched hand.

Sean had a bit of a strange accent that was a little difficult to understand. He rolled his R's, shortened words, and spoke almost too fast. It was comparable to the way Fergus spoke but much thicker. I felt like I'd heard this accent a long time ago, near the western coast I believe.

Is this the end?

He was tall with red hair and green eyes, and he seemed to be a few years older than Frank.

"Are you also an investigator?" I asked.

"Aye, been workin 'ere a wee longer than Frank. We used to be partners, we were. When I 'eard he needed help, I came runnin faster than a three-legged hog at dinner."

"We've been good friends for years, so I knew I could count on him," Frank said.

"Right, now that we're all acquainted, run us through what 'appened will ye? Sean asked.

I nodded, "Sure, no problem."

We began to walk through what happened with a quick explanation of what happened after Frank left. Once we got to the part of the story where we found the door, I walked them through each moment step by step.

When we got to the laboratory, I described everything in detail. Who the scientist was, what he was doing, and as much of his dialogue as I could remember.

"And that's when ye offed em?" Sean asked.

"No, first I threw my spear through one of the machines," I pointed at the well-decorated spear embedded in the wall. One of the guards was pulling on it, trying to separate it from the wall but he wasn't having much luck.

"Hm, I think I got it. Go on," Sean said.

So I continued to explain. We went through how I dodged under the husk and ran at Koberic, severing his arm. Then I went over his rambling and me stabbing my blade through his chest.

"So, you killed an unarmed man?" Frank asked, before quickly adding, 'No pun intended."

"He wasn't unarmed, he was in the middle of casting a spell," I explained.

"Well, I don't really blame ye," Sean said, "He was right rotten. I've never 'eard his name before, but I'll look into it."

"If he committed such an atrocity here, he probably committed others," Frank added.

By then, Aeif had already been removed from the device and was being taken out of the sewer by one of the doctors. They hadn't been able to remove the tubes yet, so they ended up cutting the tubes and taking him somewhere with better equipment.

"Right, Frank you finish up 'ere. I'm goin talk to the others."

"Sounds good," Frank replied.

Sean walked over to Reginald and Myrril and pulled them aside one at a time to talk.

"You've told us pretty much everything, but I have a few questions of my own," Frank said, "However, I think you can answer them while the doc takes a look at you."

I sighed in defeat, "I did promise you, didn't I?"

Frank waved the doctor over, "Could we have you check on his wounds? I don't know about his other ones, but his arm has me the most concerned."

"Of course," the doctor replied.

Frank asked me a few simple questions that I answered as well as I could while the doctor unwrapped the bandages on my arm. The wound was still a little tingly, but the pain was mostly gone.

"Let's see what we're wo- huh, it doesn't seem too bad," The doctor remarked.

Is this the end?

"Huh? I could have sworn it was a lot worse than that," Frank said in surprise.

The cuts on my arm weren't very deep and had already begun closing up. Frank was right, of course. The wound had been much worse a few hours ago, but it had since healed almost completely.

"It looks like I'll just have to disinfect the wound and reapply the bandages. Your arm will be all healed in a few days," The doctor commented.

"I could have sworn it needed stitches..." Frank mumbled to himself.

The doctor applied a salve of medicinal and magical herbs and re-wrapped the wound in clean bandages.

"You're all set. I'm going to go help your friends now; if you need anything just shout," The doctor said before walking over to Reginald.

I looked at Frank, "I told you it wasn't a big deal."

"But... huh?" Frank seemed to still need time, so I walked over to my spear.

The guard that had been pulling on it was now sitting against the wall, breathing heavily.

I walked up to the spear, grabbed it, and pulled it from the wall in one stroke.

The guard shot to his feet, "Wha? Um, I... I obviously loosened it for you..." He grumbled, trying to save face. As he walked off, I stored the spear back in my pocket dimension for safekeeping and convenience. Do you know how much of a hassle it is to carry around a spear all day?

I turned to Frank, "Is that all you needed me for? I'm a little tired so I'd like to get some rest."

"Huh? Oh, uh... yeah. If we have any more questions we'll drop by the Inn."

"Sounds good, I'll see you later then."

I said my goodbyes to Reginald, Myrril, and the investigators before making my way out of the rancid sewers and back to the fresh, late-afternoon air. Once I got back to The Hungry Boar, I removed my armor and let sleep take me.

Groans echoed throughout the space, seemingly sourceless. The sound of shuffling accompanied the pained voices. Darkness enveloped the world around me.

Then, a flash. I'm running, trying to escape from something. I turn behind me to see a mass of shapes shuffling in my direction.

Another flash. I'm screaming, begging them to stop. I feel their cold hands grasping at me as they slowly catch up.

Then, I'm being dragged. Dragged backward, kicking and screaming at the shapes behind me.

A flash. Countless hands run across my body, tearing into my flesh. My throat is raw from shouting, but I keep going, screaming until blood runs down my throat and bubbles in my mouth.

Darkness. Then, from the darkness come countless shapes. Faces. They look at me, study me, floating around me. Their pale, lifeless eyes bore holes through my soul, their skin grey and rotting. Arms reach out from the darkness and their hands grasp at my face.

"Repent"

Is this the end?

A voice resounds around me as fingers dig into my eyes and nose.

"Repent!"

It says once more, but with much more force.

I continued to scream as my body is pulled apart by the faces of the damned.

"REPENT!"

I jolt awake, drenched in a cold sweat. My room is dark, no light shines through the window. My heart is pounding, and my breathing is heavy.

"It's just a dream," I tell myself.

"It's just a dream..."

The next day I decided to pay Fergus a visit. His armor had helped me the day before but, to put it in simple terms, it was thoroughly trashed.

When I walked through the door to his shop, I saw Fergus lounging behind the counter absent-mindedly polishing a blade and staring out into space.

"Hey, Fergus," I approached the counter, "Got a lot on your mind?"

"Huh? Oh, Elric!" Fergus shook his head and set the blade on the counter, "Sorry about that, tis a bit slow today. Anyway, what can I do for ye?"

I dropped the bag I was carrying onto the counter.

"It's about the armor I bought here," I said.

"Oh? Ye got a problem with it?" Fergus asked, "I'll take a look."

He began to pull armor pieces from the bag and lay them

on the counter. He stroked his chin in thought as he pulled out the crushed chest plate, and snorted in surprise at the shredded vambrace.

"I don't rightfully know how ye survived a crush like this," He picked up the destroyed piece of armor, "or how yer arm ain't missing."

"I think the vambrace helped save my arm," I held up my bandaged forearm.

"Aye, that's a possibility."

"It was kind of my fault anyway, I instinctively used my arm to block a strike when I knew I needed to dodge."

Fergus shrugged, "Happens to everyone."

"I know, but that doesn't mean it wasn't a dumb mistake."

"Maybe," Fergus shrugged, "But I'm betting ye didn't come down 'ere just to talk."

I smiled, "You're right, I didn't just come here for this. I also wanted to talk about a commission."

"Oho!" Fergus's eyes lit up, "What do ye have in mind?"

"Well, I like your pre-made armor but it doesn't quite fit right, and I move around a lot so something a bit slimmer would be good," I started, "I only need vambraces, greaves, and a chest plate. Though, now that I think about it, some Faulds and Tassets I could strap to my coat would be nice."

"Aye, I could work with that. Anythin else?"

"Yeah, I don't suppose you work in Dvergen or Faerium Steel?" I asked hopefully.

Fergus raised an eyebrow, "Sorry, I've never 'eard of either of those before."

"Tsk. That's fine," I said with a deep breath, "We'll just have to go with high-grade steel."

Is this the end?

"How high?"

"As high grade as you can," I replied, "And while we're at it I might as well ask if you could imbue the steel."

"Imbue? Imbue it with what, exactly?"

I thought so. The art of imbuing metals seems to have been lost over time.

Back in Aleuria, all steel was imbued with magical energy via Bloodstones. Bloodstones are basically chunks of solid Megin. They work as a conduit for magical energy, and are very useful when making weapons and armor. It's also the base for the creation of specialized steel.

"With these," I put a bag of red gems on the counter.

"Hm?" Fergus picked one up and studied it, "Oh! I remember somethin' about the dwarves using techniques with these."

"It's not all the difficult," I explained, "Basically you use ground up Bloodstones to rebind the steel during the folding process. If you also channel Megin into the steel at the same time, you can both strengthen the steel and increase its ability to conduct magic."

"That's incredible!"

"Do you think you can do it?"

"Aye, I can give it a try for ye."

"Excellent. I would like two-millimeter steel for everything but the chest plate, which I want to be three-millimeters," I continued, "Also, I would like you to use this as an interior lining."

A small vortex of wind appeared above the counter and out dropped a rolled-up hide of black and grey.

"What an interesting spell," Fergus muttered before taking a look at the hide.

"It's direwolf, so it might be a bit difficult to cut."

"Aye, it ain't the easiest," Fergus started, "But I can work with it. Ye want this to be inside yer armor for extra protection?"

"Yes," I nodded," That and it helps pad the armor as well as keep me warm."

"I see," Fergus returned the nod, "Makes sense to me. How soon do ye need it?"

"Well, I'd say the sooner the better but I understand how hard it is to work with a new technique and so many specifications... so, how about a month?"

A smile grew across his face, "Aye, a month would be grand!"

Fergus pulled out a small measuring tape and a notepad and began to measure my arms, legs, and chest. He normally eyeballs his measurements, but this time he was being precise because I asked for a specific fit.

After a few minutes of it, he jotted down his final notes.

"Right, I'm all done 'ere. Well, other than askin what ye want to do with yer old armor," Fergus gestured to the beat-up chest plate on the counter.

"Could you sell me a replacement?" I asked.

"What for? I could have yer plate fixed up in a jiffy."

"I know, but I want to keep the dented armor."

"A reminder eh?"

I smiled, "Yeah, a reminder."

After spending quite a pretty penny at Fergus's shop, I returned to the Inn to conduct a late training session with the kids. They were really working hard, even if they

Is this the end?

weren't making drastic improvements. I really admired them for it.

Afterwards, I spent time in my room gathering my thoughts. I remembered what Myrril said about magic to raise the dead, and it still bothered me, so I pulled out the book on magic that I bought and began to flip through the pages.

It began by talking about Megin and its place in our world. The book explained how Megin was the material we expended to induce magical effects. It is something that all living creatures are born with. The amount each creature has, however, is unique.

The book stated that the easiest and most common form of magic users were called Mages. Mages used a set of magical formulae to create an effect, draining the ambient Megin from their surroundings.

This is where the book became a foreign concept to me. As far as I understood it, Megin wasn't something that could be controlled using words or images, but more of a feeling or natural intuition. Megin was, of course, the very threads that made up the fabric of our universe.

However, humans seemed to have done the impossible. They were somehow able to assign words and formulae to aspects of Megin, creating a cookie-cutter magical effect. That is what they called a Spell.

By picturing a complicated arcane sigil in their mind, a Mage would be able to speak the command word and cause the effect. Some of them even create permanent sigils for a faster casting speed.

How the hell did Humans discover something that not even the top Aleurian minds could?

I felt as if that book was understating just how amazing of a breakthrough it was.

With a single formula, any human could be a spell caster, completely changing the course of warfare forever. No longer would the Elder Races have had the upper hand with their magical combat.

I couldn't help but shudder at my new understanding of how the Elves and Dwarves lost against the humans.

My disbelief only lasted a moment as another part caught my attention. The book stated that a Mage was the most common caster. Back in my time, anyone who could control Megin and use it in combat was considered a Mage. Now, however, it seemed that there were different classifications in use.

The book didn't go into detail on what the other types were, but it did mention them from time to time. Diviners, Spiritualists, and Sorcerers were all mentioned but never elaborated on.

Most of the rest of the book explained some very basic magical formula, but I couldn't wrap my head around it at all.

"What the hell is Elemental magic?" I asked myself as I tried to understand.

Apparently, humans had not only assigned characters to Megin but also split them into different types. Every page I read made me more and more confused until I eventually found what I was looking for.

"Finally, Necromancy," I said aloud.

Necromancy was a collection of spells designed to raise and control the dead. It has various applications from medicine to exploration, such as the discovery of hidden tombs. However, the most important aspect is the ability to put ailing spirits to rest. Apparently, Necromancy was fairly important, though it was a rare skill. I didn't know how to feel about it, but the book did explain that Necromancy did not interfere with a person's soul, and did not bring them back to life. Death was, of course, the realm of the Gods.

There was also a tidbit about several incidents where a powerful Necromancer raised an army of the dead and caused great disasters, so the instruction of such magic has been restricted.

Knock. Knock. Knock.

In the middle of reading, there was a knock at the door. I let out a sigh and closed my book. At first, I was actually going to ignore it but I remembered that Frank had said they might pay me a visit.

So, I got up from bed and opened the door.

"Mr. McCloud? Do you need to ask some more questions?"

Standing outside my door was the investigator I had met the day before.

"Oh, please. Call me Sean," The investigator said, "May I come in?"

"Yeah, sure. It's a little cramped," I responded.

I stepped aside and invited him into my tiny room. He swept the room with his eyes for a moment before sitting in the chair next to the bed.

"Ye like reading?" He asked, nodding at the books.

"I do. At the moment I'm studying this one," I held up the book that was still in my hand.

"Aye, basics of magic. And we have history over 'ere."

"Yeah, I like to read," I said, "Anyway, can you answer my question?"

Sean McCloud sighed, "Aight, don't get yer trousers in a bunch. I'm not 'ere to ask more questions."

He reached into his coat and pulled out an envelope, holding it out towards me.

"I'm 'ere to give ye this."

"What is it?" I took the letter.

"An Invitation," He responded, "We're 'avin a meetin over at the Association branch to discuss the missin Husks. Yer presence would be appreciated."

I sighed, "I don't know, I don't really like this kind of thing."

"Aye, Frank told me. He also said ye would be wantin to know about the force bein put together."

"What force?"

"It's a task force for trackin down the bastards who hired that gobshite mad scientist."

I raised my eyebrow, curious. "Did you say that he was hired?"

Sean McCloud smiled, "Aye, but if ye be wanted to know more yer goin 'ave to show up to the meetin."

He got out of the chair and walked towards the door.

"Ye don't 'ave to be worrying, I'm the one runnin it."

He laughed as he patted me on the shoulder before leaving the room.

"I'll be seein ye in three days!"

CHAPTER 9

Meetings

Three days passed in what felt like moments. I had spent the time doing my usual daily activities as well as paperwork coming in from the city and from my procurement of half a logging company. To explain how that happened, we'll have to look back to before the kidnapping incident.

Edren - Three days before the kidnapping incident.

It was the afternoon and I was wandering the streets, looking for the headquarters of a company I had heard about. After asking for directions, I ended up in front of a two-story building that had seen better days.

The once vibrant yellow paint was now dull and faded. Dirt gathered in the corners and bottom of the building, and several windows are boarded up on the first and second floors. Above the rickety doors at the front of the building was a sign which read "The Hidden Grove Logging Company" in faded white letters.

The heavy door creaked loudly as I entered the totally not abandoned building. The entryway past the door was fairly dim, the only light coming from the single functioning

Necromancer's Folly

window in the front and a pair of lanterns near a long counter in the back. The room had few decorations but it was well-cleaned, partially to hide the wear on all the furniture.

I approached the counter and noticed some flyers attached to the wall just right of it. They were missing person posters. The oldest one was dated several months ago while the newest was only a few days. Each one had a crude drawing and a description of the person. It didn't take long to realize they were mostly half-elves.

"Waugh! A-A Visitor!?"

A woman jumped up from behind the desk wearing a confused face, a book in her hand. She had a soft face, on which sat a pair of reading glasses which she hurriedly tore off; her dark hair was pulled up into a bun, revealing slightly pointed ears.

"Oh, I'm sorry. I didn't mean to startle you."

"N-Not at all," She replied with a sunny smile, "We just don't get many visitors nowadays so I was surprised."

"So, what can I do for you?"

After a brief pause, she started to speak in a much more professional tone, leading me to believe she had been working as a receptionist for some time.

I returned the smile.

"I heard that this logging business wasn't doing too well," I paid no mind to the slight twitch in the woman's eye and continued speaking.

"I understand how valuable a logging business is, not only to the people of the city but to the environment as well. That's why I've come to remedy this situation."

I pulled a large bag from my pocket dimension and the

sound of clinking could be heard from within as I set it on the counter. The bag leaned over and several golden coins spilled from the top.

The woman, who probably thought it was a prank, couldn't help but yelp in surprise.

"T-This is all gold!?"

"Indeed it is."

"I-I'm sorry, I need to get the owner!"

With that sentence, the panicking young woman rushed from the room and through a door behind her.

I should probably stop surprising people to the point that they rush off in a panic, people might take it the wrong way.

As I resolved to do better, the woman returned leading an older gentleman behind her. He had a kind-looking face and short white hair and he wore small spectacles on the end of his nose. The way he carried himself led me to believe he had some kind of noble upbringing. It wasn't unusual for the second or third child of a noble to start their own businesses in a world where the firstborn inherits the title, so I was feeling good about my guess.

He approached me with a smile on his face which looked like he was trying to keep himself composed while preparing to be let down.

"Excuse me, sir. My name is Mattias Herning, and I am the owner of this establishment," The man spoke with a soft and respectful tone, "Is it true that you wish to help us with our financial situation?"

"It is."

"I see," The man's face had a hint of hope for just a moment before he let out a deep sigh, "We would be more than happy to accept your money, however..."

"Are you worried about paying it back?"

"Well, there is that..."

"Then we seem to have a bit of a misunderstanding. I am here to purchase a part of your company."

The man's eyes grew wide, "W-What? That would be incredible. All of our investors pulled out, we are in dire need of finances. But..." The air grew cold, "I'm sorry, but we cannot accept at this time."

"Hm," I couldn't help but feel like my gut had been wrong, "If I may ask, for what reason are you refusing?"

"Ah, well that's... It's not because you wish to buy a part of the company, nor is it because of the amount. You see, for some reason, the city refuses to renew our logging permit."

"Yeah, that would be a problem," I nodded.

"So you see, we cannot accept such an investment at this time. We simply can't produce profits and we're so much in the red I had to lay off most of my employees. Amy and I are the only ones left."

"It's okay Mr. Herning, I'm sure they're doing their best to approve the permit."

The receptionist, Amy, hopped in to comfort her boss.

If what he is saying is true, then investing here wouldn't be the best play. There's a low chance of them getting the permit after so long.

Mr. Herning responded to Amy, "I know you're just trying to make me feel better, but you know it as well as I that it's that damned Viden Bryher."

"We don't know that for sure."

"I can feel it in my soul. That damned man has got his finger in every city in the alliance. I'm sure he's behind this."

Oh? Now, this is getting interesting.

"Who is this Viden Bryher?"

"Huh? Oh, it um... " Mr. Herning had the look of someone who said something they shouldn't have.

"It's okay. If you tell me who it is, I may be able to help."

He hung his head, "Very well. Viden Bryher is the owner of Onforde Logging, a sort of rival business. They are based out of Onforde but Viden expanded his business to the other cities in the alliance and he has strong ties to various people in power."

"So let me get this straight. Viden Bryher expanded his company into Edren. Then, you believe he used his influence to stop your permit from being renewed so that he could rake in all the profits?"

"It's as you say," He nodded, "This is what I believe to be true."

"I see. If all we are dealing with is abusing powers and bribing officials, then I think I know of a way to fix this."

"Really?" Mr. Herning looked hopeful.

"Yes, really," I held out my hand, "My name's Elric, I look forward to working with you."

He grasped my hand, "As do I."

Mattias looked up at me with a small tear in his eye and a hopeful look on his face. I felt a little bad about taking advantage of a desperate old man, but I was also going to help him make lots of money so it evened out.

That night, a mysterious letter appeared on the Lord's desk, followed by rumors that several members of the Business Commission were arrested for bribery.

Necromancer's Folly

After all of that happened, Mattias told me that Lord Aulcrest himself visited the company to offer his apology and personally handed him the logging permit. I guess he also opened an investigation into Viden Bryher and the Onforde Logging Company.

Since then, I had spent a significant amount of time on paperwork for the reopening of the logging business. First, we had to add my name to everything and officially register me as a co-owner, then I had to help them clean up their ledgers. I was surprised to learn they still used single-entry accounting and I ended up teaching them double-entry so they wouldn't misplace as much money.

Luckily, my father had taught me a lot about managing an organization, so it wasn't too difficult for me. The hardest part was teaching Amy and Mattias about it all.

We ended up rehiring some of Mattias's old employees that he vouched for as well as a smattering of new people. I made sure to employ non-humans as well, so we had a nice smattering of races working for us.

I finished the paperwork a few hours before the meeting at the Association, so I decided to head out early to deliver it to Mattias.

"Looks like it's going to rain," I said to myself.

The sun was slowly being blocked as dark rainclouds moved in overhead; a storm was on the horizon.

As I followed the road, a yellow building slowly came into view. The two-story structure was just as faded as before, but the broken windows had been replaced and the sign was now vibrantly white. Buckets of yellow paint sat

Meetings

next to the door, the intention to repaint the building had been interrupted by the coming rain.

I pushed open the door to the brightly lit building and approached the front desk.

"Good afternoon, Sir," Amy said with a bright smile.

"Good afternoon, Amy. Is Mattias in?"

"I believe he's in his office at the moment."

"Excellent, thank you," I moved around the counter and through the door at the back.

It led into a hallway that went to side rooms on the left and right, as well as a staircase nearby. I went up the stairs and passed several empty rooms before approaching the large wooden door labeled "Mattias Herning, Owner" and knocking on it.

"Come in," A voice replied from inside.

I opened the door and entered the spacious office. Several filing cabinets ran along one of the walls while bookcases filled with ledgers ran along the other.

"Ah, Elric. What can I do for you?" Mattias asked from behind a desk covered in documents.

I pulled up a chair and sat opposite him.

"I brought the paperwork you needed."

"Ah, brilliant," he said, accepting the papers, "I was just about to ask you for these."

He grabbed a handful of other documents and put them in a folder, setting it on a stack to the side.

"So, how have these been going?" I asked.

"Pretty well," He replied. "We're going to need a few more educated employees, but we'll be fine for now."

"I did notice there were a lot of empty offices," I nodded.

"Yes," He sighed, "My former staff had already found new jobs, so I've been looking for replacements."

"I see."

"Oh! I just remembered, we also received the felling axes you ordered. But may I ask, why did you buy so many?"

"I bought a few from every smith in town," I explained, "We needed to get a feel for the best-performing axe sold at the best price."

"The concept is sound, but why not just buy from my usual guy?" He asked.

"Well, how do we know his axes are the best?" I responded with a question.

Mattias looked flabbergasted, "W-Well I.... I've used his axes for years! We've never once had a problem with their quality."

"True, I've read your ledgers."

"So why?"

"It's simple," I explained, "If we find a better axe then we'll use it, if not then we'll keep using your guy. Either way, we'll be using every axe so it won't be a waste of funds."

"Think of it as investing in a study," I continued, "We're looking for the best axe maker in town. Better equipment means they last longer, the longer they last the less money we spend in the end."

"I... I see," I started to see the wheels turning in his head, "The less money we have to keep spending on replacement equipment, the more we can put into other aspects of the business."

"Correct," I confirmed, "But don't get me wrong. We're looking for a balance between quality and price. We are not just looking to save money."

"I understand. This makes perfect sense now, thank you for explaining it to this old man." Mattias thanked me.

"It's no problem, we're partners," I replied.

We exchanged smiles before moving on to the next topic.

"Now, what did the city say about land?"

"Oh right! I have it here somewhere..." Mattias began shuffling papers around, "Ah, here it is."

He pulled out a rough diagram of the city and some of the surrounding forests. Sections of the forest were separated in outlines and labeled with a letter and a number. Three were already crossed out.

"They said we can have our pick of these four," He pointed to the plots that had been underlined.

"Any of them?" I asked.

"Yes. As an apology, Lord Aulcrest has allowed us to work on one of them for free. If we want to work on two at once, we'll have to rent the other one," He explained.

"How generous," I mumbled as I looked over the diagram.

"Well, I'd say plot A23 is a no-go," I told Mattias.

"Why is that?" He asked curiously.

"That area has been filled with Grell sightings recently, not to mention the direwolves. We would have to hire mercenaries to protect the camp, and even then It would still be pretty dangerous," I explained.

That was the part of the forest to the south of Edren where I met Reginald and Myrril. I had also studied up on the surrounding forests to make sure we made the right decision.

"Well, how about A6? That one is the most promising to

me," He pointed to a plot of land north of the city, saddled along the river.

"You aren't wrong," I nodded," It would normally be the best option. Access to the river means easy transportation. However, the only major settlement that river leads to is Onforde."

"Oh, right," Mattias's head drooped, "They don't need lumber."

"That just leaves us with A17 and B12."

"A17 is the closest, and it's not too far from the western gate of the Inner District," He pointed northwest of the city.

"True, B12 is on the western road toward Dancastle and it's a little farther from the city."

"So shall we go with A17?"

"Well, It is true that B12 is farther from the city, but it also has larger trees and more variety," I answered.

"So you want to go with B12?"

"Let's get a survey of both areas. I know the city sent its own, but it's always best to do one yourself," I said, "Though it probably won't change my mind. I think we should get both."

"Both!? That would mean spending quite a bit of money on more equipment and more manpower. I don't think we would be able to run for more than a month with our current funds!" Mattias began to panic.

"I understand what it means," I reassured him, "Sometimes you have to take risks in order to succeed."

He slumped back in his chair, "I... I just hope you know what you're doing."

So do I...

After the meeting with Mattias, I left the office and followed the directions written in the letter Sean McCloud gave me. The directions led me into the Inner District and to a two-story wooden structure with a peaked roof and clean windows. Above the double doors in the front of the building was a sign reading "The Wensworth Association for Wayward Souls".

I opened the doors and was greeted by a much different sight than I was expecting. The entranceway opened up to a hall going left and right. In front of me was a long counter reminiscent of teller's booths. Down the hall a little bit was another counter, this one larger. A sign above it indicated it was a place to buy and sell equipment and other spoils.

The area was lit by chandeliers hanging between the roof trusses, the light reflecting off the polished marble-like floor. The furniture was tasteful as were the paintings on the walls.

There didn't seem to be anyone behind either counter or sitting in the lobby.

"Elric, yer right on time."

I looked towards the voice and saw a door open to the right of the reception area. Standing there was Sean McCloud, beckoning me to follow.

"Oh good. When I saw nobody was here, I ended up thinking I was late," I said as I followed him through the door.

"We're back 'ere, in one of the meeting rooms."

Sean led me down a well-decorated hallway and up a flight of stairs before stopping in front of a set of double doors near the back of the building. A conversation could be heard from within.

He pushed open the door and walked in with confidence.

"Alright ye muppets, settle down. Elric's 'ere so we can start."

I followed after him and quickly scanned the room. In the center was a veritable smattering of odd figures seated around a circular table. Everyone shut up the moment Sean spoke and were now staring at me.

"Elric, you're over here," I looked over at the voice and saw Reginald pointing to an empty chair next to him. I made my way to the seat and sat next to Reginald, who had Myrril next to him.

"Did we really have to wait just for *him*? He doesn't look like much."

I glanced over at the one who spoke and saw a brown-haired man with his feet on the table.

"Yeah! When can we kill things!?" Next to him, a blonde man spoke up. He looked young, but his face was ever-twisted in an ear-to-ear grin and he had the eyes of a feral animal.

Across the table, a woman with dark hair and wonderful features snapped at him.

"That's just like the members of Bloody Diamond. Mes dieux, you only care about blood and death."

She spoke in such a way that made the 'th' sound more like a 'z' but her accent wasn't too heavy to understand.

"Calmez-vous, Kaelynn. We will never understand each other," the man on her left spoke to her with the same accent. He had tired eyes and dirty blonde hair, a little darker than mine.

"Right, time to shut yer gobs and listen," Sean raised his

voice to be heard. Instantly, everyone stopped speaking and looked at him.

"Since we don all know each other, I'll be introducin everyone," He continued, "Startin over 'ere we have Lorenzo Carpaccio and Smiles from the Bloody Diamond Company."

"Ciao," The brown-haired man from earlier said sarcastically.

"When do we get to fight!?" The creepy guy next to him said cheerfully.

"When we're done 'ere," Sean rolled his eyes, "By the way, where're the others from yer company?"

"They were already booked," Lorenzo sneered, picking dirt from his fingernails with a dagger

Sean put a hand to his head, "If that's true then something big is about to happen..."

He shook his head and continued, "Anyway, next up is Noirmont."

"Pardon! Why are we introduced after *them*?" the dark-haired woman interrupted with obvious contempt.

"Well Isn't this grand! We'll start with the young lass," Sean continued as if nothing happened, "She's Kaelynn Rhanes. Next to her is Karl Hoffman, and on the other side is Rodric Emmer."

The dirty blonde man nodded at the name 'Karl Hoffman' while a ginger-haired man on the other side of Kaelynn raised a brow at the other name.

"Over there's Everbrook, their leader is-"

"We can handle our own introductions," a man with slightly green skin and small tusks stood up.

Sean looked a little annoyed, but allowed it.

"The name's Fjord Tyde. This here is Azula Bleue, Fendwyr'orm, and Mikhail Ranovich."

Fjord gestured towards the people seated next to him and named them in sequence. Azula looked like a humanoid lizard with pale blue scales and a large chest. She was one of the Lizardfolk.

Fendwyr'orm was an elf, as to be expected by the name, with short blonde hair and blue eyes. I did also note that he carried two blades on his back and no sign of a bow. He must have been one of those elves that broke from tradition.

Lastly was Mikhail. He was one of the Beastfolk, a humanoid animal. He had fur covering his body and the head of a wolf.

I did find it curious that every member of their group wasn't human.

"And don't any of you dare to look down on us just because we aren't human, or we'll show you how weak you really are," Fjord finished his introductions with a threat.

Sean got back up from his seat, "Next is Lost Light. First up is Connor O'Donner,"

"It's a pleasure to meet ye," Connor was a brown-haired young man with a gentle smile and a similar accent to Sean.

"Then there's Carla Schmidt," Sean nodded toward the blonde woman seated next to Connor.

"Pleasure," She spoke in a soft voice with a slight accent that I couldn't place. It was only one word, but she seemed to pronounce it much sharper than normal and with shortened vowels.

"And Edd Jameson."

"Hello!" A hulk of a man spoke up, cheerfully. He had to have been at least seven foot tall, three hundred-fifty pounds of muscle. Light from the chandelier above the table glistened off his shiny bald head.

"We also have a special guest," Sean continued, looking at a man who was leaning against the back wall, "That is Freidrich Von Albrecht."

The room filled with gasps as all eyes focused on him.

"Who's that?" I whispered to Reginald.

"He's a One Star Mercenary, basically a legend," He whispered back.

I looked at the blonde man with a straight face up and down, but he didn't seem like a legend to me.

As Reginald later explained, the Association gave ranks to its members as a way of making sure they gave people jobs they could handle, as well as promoting competition between members.

There are six ranks within the Association:

Væng – The first and lowest rank. It's given to everyone who signs up with the association and is represented by the symbol of a single folded wing. Also called Rookies, these people make up around thirteen percent of members.
Fella Væng – The second rank. Represented by two folded wings, these Novices make up nearly twenty-four percent of members.
Svifa Væng – The third rank makes up close to thirty-nine percent of members and is represented by two open wings.
Örn – The fourth rank. If you manage to make it to this point, you are considered an expert by the Association. This is represented by a flying eagle and makes up about nineteen percent of members.
Stjarna Örn – The fifth rank. Most people cannot achieve

this rank because of their own physical limitations. Hiring someone of this rank costs an extraordinary amount of wealth and they are highly sought after by kingdoms wishing to keep them on retainer in case of invasion. They are represented by a soaring eagle with one star underneath and they make up about three percent of members.

Skínandi Örn – The sixth and final rank. These people are few and far between, with only three appearing in the last two centuries. These living legends are represented by a soaring eagle with two stars underneath. If you ever meet one, you would either be the luckiest or the unluckiest person in the world.

Just to put it in perspective, nearly everyone here is the third rank besides Fjord, who's an Örn, and Freidrich. In reality, the fourth rank is the limit of the humanoid body so the fact that Freidrich is a Stjarna Örn means he broke the limits of his body.

"Finally, we have these three," Sean continued, "Reginald Aulcrest and Myrril Delahaye, both of which are Fella Væng, and Elric um…" He turned to me, "What was your last name?"

"Tors," I said without thinking.

Sean turned back to the table, "And Elric Tors, who isn't with the association."

Damnit, I said my real name by accident!

"Hold on," Azula spoke. Her voice was feminine but also had a slight hissing sound to it, "I can understand the rank two's being here, but what's up with the nobody?"

Others in the room voiced their agreement, either not

noticing or not caring that I had the same last name as one of Edren's greatest icons.

"These three were a group, and as I understand it Elric 'ere had no problems keepin' up with the others," Sean responded, "The Association has evaluated him as at least a Fella Væng. If any of ye 'ave a problem with that, take it up with the director."

Nobody responded, but a few looked like they were thinking about complaining.

"Good, now that we're all introduced, let's get this meeting started, yeah?"

CHAPTER 10

Teams

Despite nobody talking, the tension was thick enough to cut, cook, and serve on a platter. It didn't bother me much, but Myrril looked about ready to faint.

"Right, so. Earlier in the week a young boy was kidnapped. A colleague of mine, Frank Duncan, and his partner hired Reginald and Myrril 'ere. They also asked Elric for help."

Sean went on to explain the beginning of the adventure and how we figured out where to go. He also went over the process of us figuring out it was a kidnapping ring.

"Then, they encountered some creatures they identified as husks," He put a poster on the wall behind him and pointed at it. Drawn on it was a well-made representation of the husks we encountered.

"Ha!" Lorenzo scoffed, "You had trouble with those wimpy-looking things? You should go home to your mommy, we don't need you here."

He was looking directly at Reginald, Myrril, and me.

"Hmpf, of course you judged the creature based on an image," Kaelynn spoke up.

"Kaelynn," Karl started, "It is obvious that he will not listen to you, why do you waste your energy?"

I got a feeling of déjà vu from this interaction.

"Would ye kindly shut yer yappers!" Sean yelled.

All three of them stopped talking at once.

That was when Fjord spoke up.

"I hate to say it, but he has a point."

Everyone looked a little surprised, but none more than his own teammates.

"I've seen husks before, and they aren't much of a challenge," he continued, "Sure they're faster than normal undead, but they don't have any ability that we would find concerning."

"True," Connor agreed, "We fought a few not but three months ago. The only thing ye 'ave to watch out for is gettin surrounded."

"Aye, ye would be right about that if these were normal Husks," Sean turned to my group, "Would one of ye care to explain?"

Myrril shrunk into her seat at the question while Reginald sighed, seemingly gathering his thoughts. It was then that I decided to bail them out like they had done for me.

I stood from my seat and addressed the room, "As you all know, Husks are the result of failed necromancy on a human corpse. These Husks, however, are the result of some kind of strange experiment on half-elves."

I took the moment after that statement to gauge their reactions. Lorenzo and Smiles looked uninterested, while the other humans in the room widened their eyes in surprise. The biggest reaction came from the members of Everbrook. The looks of disgust on their faces was shadowed by the anger forming on Fendwyr'orm's brow.

"I am sorry to interrupt," Freidrich, who had been listening in the back until now, had spoken. He seemed to shorten his vowels, but at the same time he pronounced them sharply. It was similar to how Carla spoke, but a bit heavier.

"Could you explain exactly why this is significant?" He asked.

I nodded," Of course. Husks have a differing amount of ability that all depends on their mutations. The more magical energy the host had, the greater the mutations."

"Dánke," said Freidrich and returned to leaning on the wall.

"To continue from that point, these Husks have a much higher ability than any you've seen before," I kept going, "They are incredibly strong, agile, and they have deadly blade-like claws growing from their fingertips."

"Pfft," Lorenzo arrogantly interrupted, "Boring. There's no way those puny claws could ever pose a danger to us *real* mercenaries."

Kaelynn opened her mouth, ready to continue their strange dynamic, but was cut off by a loud *Clang!*

All eyes fell on the object I had just tossed onto the table.

"Do you still think they aren't dangerous?" I asked as they stared at my shredded vambrace.

Smiles started to look a little less bored, but Lorenzo was still being cynical.

"Sure," he rolled his eyes, "They cut through some cheap metal, so what?"

A hand reached out and picked up the vambrace. I looked to see Roderic closely inspecting it. This was the first time he had done anything other than listen.

Teams

"I see..." His voice was deep and his accent thick, but I could just about understand what he was saying.

"Vous vous trompez, this is not cheap metal," He continued speaking, mixing in his native language in a way that made me think he wasn't fluent in the common tongue, "This is bonne qualité, very good metal."

He set the vambrace back onto the table and went back to being quiet. It seemed that, although he didn't say much, what he did say was highly valued since even Lorenzo looked like he accepted it.

"Right," Sean stood back up, "While yer 'ere, we might as well have ye explain the other one, yeah?"

He placed another poster next to the first one. This one depicted a much bigger form, reminiscent of the large Husks we fought. As soon as he put it up, Lorenzo leaned forward with a look of interest.

"Okay, this one is another kind of Husk we encountered. This one is much larger and much more-"

"This one is more mutated," Fendwyr'orm interrupted. He didn't have an accent or a particular way of speaking. This was a phenomenon that all full-blooded elves were capable of, to every person in this room it sounded like he was speaking their native language. "Does that mean these are..."

I made eye contact with him and nodded, "I'm sorry, the large husks used to be elves."

He averted his eyes as his face distorted in anger, his hands clenched so tight his knuckles were white.

There was a stereotype that said elves were a race of people without emotion, or that they suppressed their emotions. This was completely wrong. Elves felt emotion the same as any of us, they just don't like to show it to outsiders. I wasn't sure if this was the same nowadays, but to me seeing an elf lose control of their emotions in front of strangers was enough to tell me how much pain he was in.

I took a deep breath and continued, "These large Husks have limb mutations that vary, with some having every limb enlarged while others having none and everything in between," I placed my crushed chest plate on the table, "This was caused by one of them charging at full speed. I had also braced myself at the time, but the Husk hit me with enough force to send me into a wall."

"We really recommend ye not get hit by em," Sean chimed in, "Khris Lockemor, Frank's partner, got smacked by the bugger and broke nearly every bone in his chest."

Lorenzo and Smiles eyes were lit up like fireworks. *They must really like to fight dangerous things,* I guessed.

"Oh, and one more thing," I said, "Both of these types of Husks also have something in common. They're intelligent."

"WHAT!?"

They yelled in surprise, with Mikhail letting out a growl and Azula a hiss. They started talking over each other, yelling and arguing about the prospect of intelligent undead. It was loud enough that not even Sean could calm them down immediately. The only ones not shouting were Freidrich, who had his eyes closed in thought, and the few of us who already knew about this.

"That's enough!"

Sean's voice echoed through the room, the arguing dying down.

Mikhail, the Beastfolk, looked Sean in the eyes and said, "Are you sure they are intelligent?"

The way he spoke was methodical, sounding out every syllable in a sort of growl. Beastfolk had a different way of speaking than we do, a lot of our sounds don't exist in their language so it's harder for them to learn and speak the common tongue than most of us. Though, many Beastfolk were able to speak as fluently as a native speaker.

"Aye," Sean nodded, "Elric was the one to realize it when the Husk he was fighting tried to do a feint."

"Hm," Mikhail gave an acknowledgment.

"I would like to ask something," Connor started, "I was under the impression that ye killed all of these Husks, so why are we bein told all of this?"

"That's simple. We didn't get 'em all."

"Yes, we believed all of these husks were the people that had gone missing recently, so we think there should be around fifty more," I added.

Sean gave me an approving look, but I still felt dumb for speaking like I was running the meeting. I guess old habits die hard.

"Heh... Hehe," Smiles began to giggle creepily, "There's mooorrrre? Oh goodie!"

Every time he spoke, I felt a chill shoot up my back. I had a feeling this guy would kill me without any hesitation...

"Aye, but before ye go on a rampage, ye should know they're only 'alf the story," Sean said.

Now I was interested as well. I remember he said the crazy scientist whose name I had forgotten had been hired by somebody and I was hoping this information was next.

"When we were searchin the sewer lab, we found a few letters detailing instructions for Koberic as well as promises of payments and details on finding test subjects," Sean continued, "We also found bloodstones filled with necromantic magic attached to his strange machines."

"So, we are looking for a necromancer?" Freidrich asked from the back of the room.

"The ones who hired him and the necromancer who filled the bloodstones may not even be working together," Fjord said.

"Hmpf, I find it more likely that this necromancer and the ones who hired le scientifique are working together, no?" Kaelynn added.

"Of course someone of the Elfbane would disagree with a 'non-human'," Fendwyr'orm spat.

Elfbane? What the hell is that supposed to mean?

"You still call us that even though it's been nearly eight-hundred years since the genocide of the elves?" Karl sneered, "Putain! This is what's wrong with the long-lived races, they never let anything go."

Fendwyr'orm looked about ready to kill Karl but a large, furred hand grabbed his shoulder.

"It is not worth it, my friend," Mikhail said to him.

Fendwyr'orm reluctantly sat back in his seat, but continued to glare at Karl.

"I agree with Kaelynn," Azula said, "It is much more likely that they are working together. It is cleaner that way."

"That was our thought as well, lass," Sean nodded.

"So... we're looking for a necro-whatzit?" The way Edd asked the question made me realize he wasn't the sharpest tool in the toolbox.

"Necromancer," Carla corrected him.

"Right, sorry..." Edd looked a little sheepish when he was corrected. It was hard to believe he was a mercenary.

"Yer right, Edd. One of the letters detailed a large ceremony being conducted soon. We think it's either today or tomorrow."

"Oh cool, we get to search for a necromancer that could be anywhere in the city in order to stop some kind of ceremony. Also want us to kill a god while we're at it?" Reginald asked sarcastically.

"Cut the sarcasm, Aulcrest," Sean snapped, "I know it won't be easy, but that's why all of ye are 'ere."

So he did say Aulcrest. Does that mean Reginald is the son of the Lord? He has to be related in some way, at the very least. I didn't see him there when I planted that letter for Mattias, but that doesn't mean much.

"I'm going to agree with the rich brat. There's no way we can find a single guy in a city of seventy thousand, and I'm not much of a searching kind of guy. Vaffanculo!" Lorenzo said with a bit of malice.

Sean let out a heavy sigh, "Listen 'ere; I've had it just about up to 'ere with yer-"

"I have an idea," I interrupted.

Sean stopped mid-sentence and glared at me, "This best be good, I'm in no mood to be playin around."

"Well," I gulped, "I assumed you were going to try and narrow down where the necromancer could do a large ceremony in secret. I'm guessing you already ruled out the main city and are looking at the inner district."

"That would make sense," Freidrich started, "the inner district has a lot of large buildings that could be rented or bought, if you had friends in high places."

"Yes, exactly," I continued, "I bet you were also going to have us look around the sewers to see if more of those Husks are around, and try to follow them to their source like we did before."

"Aye, but is there a point to this Mr. Tors?" Sean looked irritated.

"Sorry, yes. I remember reading about necromancers recently," I said, finally getting to the point, "The passage said that necromancers aren't inherently evil, and they are used for a whole lot of things."

"Y-Yes!" Myrril yelled, then instantly shrunk back into her chair, "I-I m-mean... um... n-necromancers are used for s-stuff like... finding l-lost t-tombs..."

"Myrril got it," I said, "I was wondering if the necromancer wasn't going to be in the Tomb of the Fallen?"

"The Tomb of Fallen?" Sean asked.

"Yeah, the large catacomb where the lords of the city and their knights are interred," I explained.

"Sorry, Elric. Edren doesn't have any catacombs," Reginald said.

"What!?" I said, a little surprised, "That's impossible. A Tomb of the Fallen is built in every Aleurian city!"

"He speaks the truth," Freidrich calmly chimed in.

Roderic nodded, "I have been to a few Aleurian villes, they each had one."

"Okay, just because other Aleurian cities have them, doesn't mean *this* one does," Reginald turned to me, "Why are you so sure it's here?"

I wracked my brain for something to say since I couldn't just tell him I had visited it once when I was a kid.

"Okay, I'll give you three reasons," I said confidently, "First, Edren was first conquered by Wolfram, The One Man Army. He was a legend, even while he was alive. He got administration of the city given to one of his sons, who the people loved. There's no way they wouldn't have made a Tomb of the Fallen."

"Second, Edren was at the center of a major trade route much like it is now. It was imperative for not only defense, but for getting supplies out to the front line. It could be said that the Aleurian expansion east wouldn't have been possible without Edren."

I smiled, "The third reason is a lot simpler. Building a Tomb of the Fallen is an Aleurian tradition for all settlements large enough to be called a city and personally administrated by a noble."

Reginald looked at me in disbelief, "That's it? That's your third reason? Edren was taken as an Aleurian city near the end of the Empire, how are you so sure they didn't skip tradition considering their country was falling apart!?"

I looked him dead in the eyes and said, "I've dedicated my life to understanding the Aleurian culture and traditions. Trust me, they wouldn't have shirked on their tradition even if the gods were descending upon them."

"Wha-"

Reginald started to say something but Sean interrupted.

"I'm convinced."

"Really?" Reginald asked.

"So are we," Fjord said.

Reginald sighed and put a hand to his head.

"Right, that helps a lot," Sean continued, "So, ye need to look for this catacomb somewhere in the Inner District. It will probably be crawling with Husks and whatever the Aleurians left behind. I'll be putting you all in teams, so-"

"Finally, a real challenge!" Lorenzo jumped to his feet,

"Come on smiles, we get to fight those husks while dodging genuine Aleurian traps! Is this heaven or what?"

"Hehehehehe!" Smiles giggled as he and Lorenzo rushed out of the room.

"Wait! We're making teams first...." He sighed, "Whatever, this will make things easier for all of us."

He turned back to all of us.

"Right, I'll be putting Noirmont and Everbrook together since ye probably won't kill each other. Is that alright with ye?"

The members of both groups nodded.

"Grand! That means I'll 'ave Lost Light pair up with these three if you don't mind."

"We don't mind," Connor responded.

Reginald, Myrril, and I didn't mind either, so it was set.

"And Freidrich will be workin alone as usual."

Freidrich nodded from the back.

"Now then. We 'ave our teams, now it's time to get looking. There could be an entrance to the tomb anywhere. In the sewers, behind a house, inside a building, anywhere. Make sure ye search carefully and report back when ye find it."

We all nodded.

"Good. Then get goin, and may the Gods watch over ye."

CHAPTER 11

Lost Light

As we all began shuffling out of the Association building, the members of Lost Light approached us in the reception area. Connor had a big smile on his face, Carla looked uninterested as usual, and Edd seemed to be deep in thought.

"I'd like to properly introduce ourselves," Connor said, "My name is Connor O'Donner, next to me is Carla Schmidt, and the big lug 'ere is Edd Jameson. Looks like we'll be workin with ye for a bit."

I shook his outstretched hand, "Pleasure to meet you. I'm Elric, and these are my companions, Reginald and Myrril."

"So, do ye 'ave any idea where we should start lookin?" He asked.

"Well, the most likely place would be the Inner District. The Aleurians tended to build the Tomb of the Fallen in the most fortified location." I responded.

"Sounds like a plan to me, how about ye?" He turned to look at his companions.

Carla just shrugged like it wasn't her problem, and Edd nodded enthusiastically.

"I wanna see the castle!" Edd said, nodding like a maniac.

"We think the Inner District is a good place to start as well," Reginald said, with Myrril hiding behind him.

"Wow, this is already going well," I mused.

"Shall we?" Connor asked, gesturing us to lead the way.

Just as we started towards the door, a voice called out from behind.

"Hold up, Elric!"

I turned to see Sean jogging up to me.

"Huh? Did I forget something?" I asked.

"No, not at all. It was me who forgot to give ye this," Sean pulled a small circular object from his pocket, similar to the ones Reginald and Myrril have.

"What's this?"

"It's an Association Medal," he explained, "It's meant to let customers know who ye are. The Director had it made, probably in an effort to get ye to join."

"Ah. Thanks, but no thanks," I replied.

I really had no interest in getting attached to the Association. I still had no idea who they were or what their true intentions were. They seemed to be a semi-altruistic organization, but I had a feeling that it was just a façade.

Sean sighed, "Look, I don't know why ye don't want to join the Association and I really couldn't care less, but the Medal can come in handy. For instance, they won't charge ye at the gate to the Inner District if ye show it to them."

It was my turn to sigh, "Alright, but I'm not joining."

Sean smiled, "I wasn't asking ye to, that's something the Director will 'ave to ask ye himself if he wants ye that bad."

I took the medal from Sean and looked it over. The entire thing was made from polished metal. The front was a carved image of folded wings suspended in the center of a circle. Small words were carved around the edge that read "The Wensworth Association for Wayward Souls". And at the very bottom, underneath the wings, it simply said "Fella Væng".

On the back was written a bit of information, seemingly allowing the medal to act as a form of identification in the event of your death, and a strange series of numbers. It looked something like this:

Name: Elric Wolfram Tors

Age: 19

Race: Human

Rank: Fella Væng

City of Registry: Edren, Valtion-Silma City State Alliance

00|01|00|1|1135

"What in Kyrtvale!? How does the Director know my full name? I haven't told anybody here." I calmed my thoughts and decided to look into it at a later date.

I shoved the Medal into my pocket and looked back at Sean, "Thanks."

"No problem," he replied, "I wish ye all luck out there."

"So... While we're walking, I'd like to get to know a bit more about you guys," Reginald asked while we trudged through heavy rain that had started while we were inside.

"Go for it," Connor said, "I've got a few questions myself."

"Okay, um... first I guess, can I ask where you're all from?" Reginald asked.

"I'm from a small town on the western coast of the Dolar

Imperium," Connor started, "Carla 'ere doesn't know where her parents are from, but she grew up in a town at the base of the Norduff Mountain Range to the north."

"And what about Edd?"

"We're not too sure about him. As ye probably guessed, he ain't the brightest," he explained, "But he's still a valued member of our team."

"What about all of ye?" He asked.

"Oh, Myrril and I have lived here all our lives," Reginald replied.

"Is it true that yer really the son of the lord?" Connor asked.

Reginald sighed, "Yes, it is. I really don't like to tell people because then they start treating me differently."

"Ah, I understand," Connor looked at me, "What about ye, where're ye from?"

"West," I replied, "Well, south-west. I basically grew up on the coast."

"Ye grew up on the coast as well? Finally, someone who understands me," Connor chuckled, "The weather is hard to get used to, yeah?"

I nodded, "It's not humid enough for my liking."

"Ye really are from the coast!" Connor said cheerfully.

"I have a question now," I said, "Why did you become a mercenary?"

"Hm," Connor seemed to think for a moment, "I suppose it's because I wanted to help people. That's the reason we formed Lost Light."

"You're pretty," I heard from behind me.

I turned to see Edd trying to talk to Myrril as she attempted to hide from our new companions.

"N-No I'm n-not..."

"Yes, you are," Edd said, "If I think you're pretty, then that means you're pretty."

Edd spoke in a tone that made it seem a little like he was pouting and a lot like what he said was matter-of-fact.

I was about to say something when I saw Myrril start creeping out from behind Reginald. Apparently, Edd's way of speaking somehow got Myrril to start warming up to him. Maybe it was because he acted similar to a child so Myrril didn't feel as nervous around him.

"So Elric," Connor continued, "Why don't ye want to join the Association?"

I thought about my answer for a moment. Connor had asked a question that was hard to talk about to members of the Association.

"Honestly, I just don't trust it," I answered.

"How so?"

"Well, I know next to nothing about them," I explained, "I don't know who runs it, where the money goes, or even if their intentions are pure. I'm skeptical that they just want to help people find a place to fit in."

"So ye thing they 'ave some hidden motivation?" He asked.

"Yeah, sorry if that offends you."

"Not at all. In fact, I somewhat agree with you. No company gets that big without a few dark dealin's."

Satisfied with his statement, I decided to go back to my previous question.

"What about you, Carla? Why did you become a merc?" I asked the lady giving me a cold shoulder.

She sighed, "Our conversing is not necessary for this operation."

"Oh don't be like that Carla, just answer the man," Connor said.

"Fine," She replied, "I became a merc in order to find my parents."

"Have you had any luck?" Reginald asked.

She shook her head.

"Now that I think about it, I don't know why you became a merc," I directed the implied question at Reginald.

He shrugged, "I'm the second son, I'm basically a backup for my older brother. I wanted to find something worthwhile to do with my life."

"And Myrril?" Connor asked.

"She said she made a promise with someone, but wouldn't tell me much more than that," he replied.

A moment later, we arrived at the gate to the Inner District. Just like Sean said, we showed the guard our Association Medals and they let us through without any hassle. I told myself to thank Sean again once I saw him.

"All right, now that we're 'ere, where should we be lookin?" Connor asked.

"I would say around the central hill. The castle in the middle of the old city is the most fortified place," I started, "But it wouldn't be inside the castle since the entrance was restricted. That means it will be somewhere near the base."

"Sounds good to me."

We began to search the base of the hill for any sign of the Tomb. I couldn't actually remember the exact location, but I had the general idea of where it was and was guiding everyone that way, slowly but steadily.

In the meantime, we started chatting again.

"If we're going to be fighting together, it's probably best if we know each other's combat capabilities," I said.

"True," Connor agreed, "I'm a bit of an up-close fighter."

He patted a short sword hooked on his left.

"So am I, but I use a longword," I placed my hand on the sword hanging from my hip, "Reginald's also for the front. He uses a kite shield and broadsword."

"I-I use magic..." Myrril piped up.

"I see," Connor said, "Then you're rearguard like Carla. She uses a bow."

"And Edd is front lines as well, yes?" Reginald asked.

"Mhm," Connor nodded, "He uses his fists."

"So we have two in the rearguard and four in the vanguard," I analyzed.

"At least it's not the other way around," Connor chuckled.

Then, a thought occurred to me.

"You guys have been in the Association a long time yeah? Could someone explain what the weird numbers are on the back of my Medal?" I asked.

"Hm? Oh, those things. They're actually pretty simple," Reginald started," The first number indicates how many jobs you've accepted from the Association, the second is how many you've completed, and the third is how many you've failed."

"And the rest?"

"The next number is just to indicate if you work in a group or not. A one is a yes and a zero is a no," Reginald explained, "And the final set is just your registration number. Apparently, they file people's profiles based on their number instead of their name."

"Huh, I guess that makes sense," I said, but there was still something bothering me.

Why does it say I've completed a job even though I've never accepted one?

When I asked Reginald, he said, "I'm not sure, I've never seen it before."

"Maybe you completed a job without knowing it," Connor suggested.

What Connor said made sense, but it still felt strange. It was yet another thing I would have to think about at a later date.

A large chamber – Somewhere underneath Edren.

A man stood hunched over an opened sarcophagus in the center of the torch-lit room, the lid sitting off to the side. He had slick black hair, round glasses, and a wild look in his eyes. He wore a gray robe decorated with various charms and precious metals.

"Lord Kane!" Another man in grey robes approached, "We have reports of intruders within the tomb."

A smile stretched across Kane's face.

"So, we have finally been found."

He spoke in a soft and intelligent manner that betrayed the crazed look on his face.

"What should we do, my lord?" The other man asked.

Kane, continuing his work, replied, "We will do nothing."

"Nothing, sir?"

"Yes," Kane said, "There is no need to worry. The protectors of the tomb will take care of them long before I'm finished here."

The other man bowed and back away into the darkness.

Kane refocused on his work. In front of him was a mummified corpse, laying peacefully in the sarcophagus. Wisps of dark-blonde hair were atop its head, and it was dressed in the most amazing robes Kane had ever seen. A treasure trove of personal artifacts and precious materials sat all around it. And embedded in various places along its skin were small, red stones.

Kane began to hum to himself as he placed another stone, and another. Each time, a small amount of magical energy surged into the corpse.

"It won't be long now, Lord of Edren."

Kane let out a chuckle, and went back to his work.

We continued talking for a while, ignoring the odd looks we were getting from the residents of the Inner District as we searched for the Tomb of the Fallen.

Eventually, we came upon some kind of disturbance. A large crowd had gathered around a spot at the base of the hill, whispering to each other. A couple of guards were trying to calm everyone down.

"Keep it civil people, there's nothing to worry about!" One of the guards shouted, which just seemed to upset the people even more.

"What do you mean there's nothing to worry about!" One of the people shouted.

"Yeah!" Another said, "One minute I was minding my own business, and the next stones were flying through the air!"

"We could have been hurt, or worse!" A woman screamed.

The crowd shouted in agreement.

"I understand your concerns, we sent a message to the castle and are waiting for a response," the guard from before responded in a calm tone, "We just ask you to be patient while we figure this out."

"Be patient!?" A lady sounded offended.

"Are we under attack?"

"Is it the Abnormals!?"

"Did the Imperium finally invade!?"

Questions began to fly around as the crowd became more agitated.

"Let's check it out guys," I said to the others.

"It's not our job to take care of civil disturbances," Reginald said, a little annoyed.

"I agree with Elric," Connor jumped in, "This may be what we're lookin for."

I approached the crowd and began pushing through, till I made it to the front.

"Excuse me," I asked the guard, "What's going on here?"

The guard looked at me, "Nothing to be worried about, sir."

I looked behind him and saw a jagged hole in the side of the hill. Behind it, I could faintly see the appearance of masonry, very old and familiar masonry.

"Sorry Mr. Guard, but this is what we're looking for," I pushed past the guard, followed by the others.

"W-Wait, you can't just-"

"It's alright, we're with the association," Reginald detached his Medal from his chest plate and held it up to the protesting guard.

After that, the guard seemed to give in. Either he trusted the Association, or he was too scared of our fighting strength to try and remove us.

"A-Are you s-sure this is it?" Myrril asked.

I nodded, "I'm sure, look at that."

The masonry that started near the entrance to the hole continued further into the darkness. A frame of stone sat a little ways in, with massive granite doors engraved with damaged images of Aleurian warriors. Strangely, they were partially open.

"Wow..." Carla whispered.

"So cool!" Edd said with glee.

"It is," Connor said, "But how do we know this is the actual tomb and not some other ruin?"

I pointed at the top of the door frame, "Those characters are at the entrance to all of the other tombs, so it has to be."

The characters I had pointed to were actually Aleurian script that read "Tomb of the Fallen", but I couldn't just tell them that's what it said.

Connor nodded, "Good enough for me."

I went back to the guard and informed him of the situation. He was surprised but seemed to understand the situation.

"So you see, we need you to send a message to the Association. If you could also get some more guards to make sure nobody comes or goes, that would be awesome," I said.

He nodded, "I understand, but what should we do about the crowd?"

"I'll handle this," I put my hand on his shoulder to reassure him before turning to the growing mob.

"If I could have your Attention, please!" I used a bit of Megin to project my voice so I could be heard over the rain, "We have just discovered an ancient Aleurian Tomb in the hillside."

A cacophony of whispers began to spread through the crowd.

"Do not fear. We are from the Association and have been tasked with securing the ruins," I continued, as sighs of relief could be heard, "However, we ask you to not attempt to approach or enter the Tomb at this time. Aleurians secured their Tombs with dangerous magics, and anyone that enters unprepared will most likely not return."

I finished by saying, "We have called in additional reinforcements in an excess of caution. As long as you stay clear of the entrance, you are perfectly safe."

The people began talking amongst themselves, but the tension in the air was dissipating.

"Are you sure it was okay to tell them all of that?" The guard asked.

"He did good," Reginald replied, "People fear what they do not understand. Elric took the unknown out of the equation, so the people can feel more at ease."

"I see," The guard nodded, "I did feel better once he told me what was happening."

"Good, then make sure none of the civilians approach, "I

said, "I'm not sure how safe even being in front of the doors is."

The guard's face drained as I turned and walked back toward the Tomb.

"That was amazin," Connor told me, "I've never felt charisma like that, it even made me feel better."

I shook my head, "Anyone could have said it and it would have had a similar effect."

"Don't sell yourself short," Reginald placed a hand on my shoulder, 'You may have just averted a riot. I only know a few people who could do that with just a few words."

I was starting to feel a little uncomfortable with all the praise.

"It was nothing, really," I said, "Anyway, shouldn't we be going in now?"

I started walking toward the doors.

"Sh-Shouldn't we wait f-for the others?" Myrril asked.

"There are six of us, I think we'll be fine," I replied.

Reginald chimed in to reassure her, "Besides, if it gets too dangerous we can always wait to proceed."

Myrril nodded, "O-Okay…"

With that, we slipped through the open door and entered the dark catacombs beneath Edren.

CHAPTER 12

Tomb of the Fallen

It was pitch black once we shut the heavy doors behind us, prompting the lighting of several torches. We were in the entrance hall of the Tomb. Braziers lined the walls between faded murals depicting various scenes from history. Cobwebs hung from the arched ceiling, and dust filled the musty air. The floor was made of beautiful white marble that still had a slight polish and most importantly, it was dry.

I welcomed the familiar Aleurian architecture as the rest of the group looked around, wonder in their eyes.

"Woah, this place is amazing," Reginald mused.

"It is," I nodded.

"Hey Elric," Connor called, "Are these murals in every Tomb of the Fallen?"

"Yes," I said, "But they are each personalized for the city the tomb is built in."

"S-So nobody's seen t-these in over a thousand y-years?" Myrril asked.

"It would seem that way."

I responded to Myrril almost on autopilot. The last time I was here, I watched an artist painting one of these murals, and seeing them again was a burst of nostalgia I should have been ready for.

"I think this is the way forward," Carla called from a set of doors at the far end of the room.

I snapped out of my reminiscing and responded, "It looks like the only way we can go."

Connor approached the doors and gently pushed them open, which let out a loud creak that echoed through the chamber.

"It's a staircase," He said after glancing through the doorway.

We started down the staircase two at a time, with me and Connor taking the lead and Reginald and Edd at the rear.

"So, Mr. Aleurian expert," Connor began, "What should we be expecting down 'ere?"

"Well, we should at least expect traps," I replied, "Aleurian traps are usually magical by nature, but they've been known to use physical traps as well."

"I see," He nodded, "And do you think there'll be Husks?"

I shrugged, "I have no clue."

"Myrril. I don't like the dark..." Edd said behind us, sounding scared.

"I-It's okay Edd," Myrril responded, "I-I'll protect y-you."

It was so weird hearing Myrril reassuring someone, and even weirder to see her smiling at him, like she was enjoying it.

After another moment, we reached the bottom of the stairs and entered the first burial room. I said room, but it was more of a hallway. There were cubbies dug into the walls on either side where the bodies of warriors would be interred.

Connor lit a brazier next to the entrance which lit up a portion of the room. Instantly, we all realized something was wrong.

"By the Gods..." I murmured as I set eyes on the state of the room.

"Why are the dead people on the floor?" Edd asked.

That was the question we were all asking.

The cubbies on the walls were all empty, instead, the bodies that should have been there were scattered around the room. Some were slumped against the wall, others were face down on the ground. What all of them had in common was the ancient armor they wore, they all had weapons in their hands, and they all looked like they had been hacked and slashed repeatedly.

"By the Goddess!" I shouted as the answer hit me.

"What? What is it?" Connor asked.

I turned to everyone, "I think these are Draugr, Warriors tasked with guarding their Lords even in death."

"WHAT!? Why didn't you say anything earlier!?"

"I-I'm sorry," I stuttered, "I thought they were myths!"

"This complicates things," Carla said.

"Yeah it does! Who wants to fight undead Aleurians?" Reginald shouted.

"Um...." Edd started, "Why are they all dead?"

Everyone froze. We simultaneously realized that we had glossed over a very important fact, and yet Edd had been the one to focus on it. We looked at each other, our eyes asking the question "Why *are* they dead?".

"Someone must have arrived before us," Connor said.

"O-Or they aren't a-actually dead..." Myrril mumbled.

We all froze once again and quickly jumped into a

defensive formation, with the long-range members behind us. After a moment of nothing happening, I approached one of the face down Draugr and poked it with my sword.

"It's okay, I'm pretty sure they're really dead," I called out, prompting everyone to relax a little bit.

Carla let out a sigh, "I was not in the mood to be ambushed by the dead."

"Now this just leaves the question of who killed them," I said.

"Do you think it was the necromancer?" Connor asked.

I shook my head, "No, I'm guessing the Necromancer somehow took control of them. If he didn't, then he would have once they were dead. Even Undead, Aleurians would be a fearsome enemy."

"So it must have been one of the other groups, right?" Reginald asked.

"Probably," I nodded.

Connor sighed, "Our best bet is to follow the path of carnage and meet up with em."

I could have sworn I also heard him mutter, "Gods I hope it's not Bloody Diamond."

"Then let's keep going," Carla said.

"Yeah, just don't lower your guard. The others could have missed some," I added.

I had noticed that Carla was speaking more, but I wasn't sure If it was her nerves or if she had just gotten more comfortable around us.

Anyway, we started down the hallway and continued through into another chamber, this one also filled with dead bodies... well, re-dead bodies. After that, we came to a circular chamber with three branching paths, and several more unmoving Draugr.

"Tsk. Now which way?" Connor said to nobody in particular.

"We should just keep going straight," Reginald said.

"No," Carla disagreed, "We should go right."

"Left!" Edd chimed in, thinking it was some kind of game.

I decided to speak up, "It doesn't matter which way we go. If this is like all the other Tombs, then each path leads to the main burial chamber."

"H-How do you k-know t-that's where we n-need to go?" Myrril mumbled.

I shrugged, "If I were a necromancer, I would base myself with the strongest dead to raise."

"Which way do ye think then?" Connor asked.

"Well, the central path is the shortest," I started.

"Ha!" Reginald said triumphantly.

"But," I continued, "If you look closer, you'll see the chamber through the central doors has collapsed."

"Oh..." Reginald looked disappointed.

"Like I said, we should go right!" Carla said as she approached the doors on the right.

"Wait a second," She said in surprise, "There's no door here, It's just a solid wall!"

"Ah, it was probably the next part to be dug out..." I told her.

I remembered the right wing not being built when I had visited as a kid, but I had assumed they had gotten to it, but I guess not.

"Looks like we're going with the left," Connor said.

"Yay!" Edd shouted.

We followed behind Edd as he happily skipped away down into the left wing of the Tomb.

"Edd, just be careful, yeah? There may be traps 'ere and I don't want ye-"

Connors' warning was cut short by a bright flash of light and the sound of meat hitting stone.

"EDD!" Carla yelled, her voice tinged with fear.

"Owie..."

As the light faded from our eyes we saw Edd slumped against the wall, a slightly smoking scorch mark on his chest.

"Edd, are ye alright?" Connor asked, rushing over to him.

"I smell like bacon," Edd said with a giggle.

Connor sighed, "Yeah, yer alright."

After that, we decided to keep Edd in the back and have me and Connor take up the front again. I was shocked that Edd was still alive after getting hit with a bolt of lightning, but I was even more surprised that he just kept going like nothing happened.

It took me a moment to get over the surprise, but I was soon back to focusing on the task at hand.

As we moved forward, keeping an eye out for any physical traps or strange runes on the floor and walls, I started thinking about the other groups. I knew next to nothing about them, but I still found myself debating which one would be better to run into down here.

Eventually, I just decided to ask the others to fill me in.

"The other groups?" Connor asked, "How do ye not kno- oh right, yer not with the Association. Sure, I can help."

"Thank you."

"How about we start with Freidrich," Connor said, "He doesn't belong to a group or company, so he's what we call a Loner."

As he explained it, Loners were people who decided to complete jobs alone for whatever reason. Plenty of people are loners, but only a few of them are ever successful. Freidrich is one of them, and one of the highest-ranked members of the Association. He's destroyed countless dangerous monstrosities and rid the world of numerous beasts and Abnormals, but none of those were his greatest achievement. For that, he single-handedly killed a swarm of wyverns before taking on, and defeating, a dragon.

"That's impressive," I said with genuine shock.

"Yeah, it really is. You can count the people in history who 'ave singlehandedly killed a dragon on one hand," Connor responded.

"Who's next?" I asked.

"Everbrook, "Connor answered, "Fjord is the leader, and as you could probably tell, he's a half-orc. He's a decent guy, but he always thinks that everyone's out to get him because he's not human."

Connor described Everbrook as a group of non-humans who fight to prove to the world that they are just as capable, or better, than humans. He also said that they are probably just in it to make tons of money. They take on extremely dangerous jobs in order to prove their worth, but they also make quite the paycheck. Connor seemed skeptical about their motives.

Next, he talked about Noirmont. They were a small

group of people based near the foot of the Black Mountain in The Faeron Kingdom. They prefer fighting abnormal creatures and hunting beasts rather than killing people, but they aren't strictly opposed to it. They have a long list of achievements but don't like to brag about them. Connor also said that they're the most reasonable of all the groups we met earlier.

"The only one left was Bloody Diamond, right?"

Connor groaned at my question, "Man, I was hopin ye forgot about em."

"They were the most memorable ones at the meeting," I said.

"Yer not wrong," Connor sighed.

At this time, we had just passed through another hall and were beginning to carefully make our way down a staircase, lighting torches and braziers as we went.

"Bloody Diamond is a mercenary company with around one hundred members," Connor explained, "Though, only seven of them are considered the best. They're the ones ye need to watch out for. They made a name for themselves through bloody conquest in various wars throughout Vestri, and-"

"Sorry to interrupt, but where is Vestri?" I asked.

Connor looked surprised.

"Ye don't know the name of the continent yer on?" He raised his brow.

I shook my head, "Sorry, maybe I know of it by another name."

"Ah, got it," He nodded, "Anyway, Bloody Diamond had a hand in most wars in Vestri, the western continent, that occurred during the last fifty or so years. The most recent one would be the Frosthaven incursion around five years ago."

"I see," I nodded, "And were Lorenzo and Smiles involved as well?"

"Yeah," Connor said, "From what I've 'eard, they were front runners for spots in the top seven when the war happened. Afterward, they were accepted into the fold."

Connor paused for a moment before continuing, "I've also 'eard it's where Smiles got his name."

"I figured it wasn't his real name."

"Yeah well, apparently during the war he fought an entire regiment of soldiers himself. They say that his smile never faded no matter how many men he cut down."

I felt a shiver go up my spine. Not many people could claim to take on a regiment of trained soldiers by themselves, and even fewer would do it with a smile. It was then I realized that Smiles was a truly demented man.

"Since then, they've terrorized so many. It's actually surprising that they don't have a bounty on their he- Speak of the devil," Connor paused as we reached the bottom of the stairs, the dim torchlight just barely lighting up a figure. Their ear-to-ear grin and cold eyes stared directly at us.

"Right, so it was yer team who made it 'ere before us," Connor called out.

Smiles gave no reply. He just stood there, staring at us.

"So now you're ignoring us?" Reginald said, annoyed.

Smiles didn't so much as flinch. That's when I noticed something, a sound in the darkness. It was almost like shuffling feet, or the sound someone makes when getting into a stance, but Smiles had yet to move.

"It's an ambush!" I yelled.

Everyone dropped into a stance, preparing for Lorenzo and smiles to come charging at us. I wasn't going to wait.

I held my hand out and channeled my inner Megin into my arm while imagining the light of the sun. Not but an instant later a bright light appeared in the form of a small ball hovering in front of my palm. Its warmth filled the staircase and the room at the bottom, giving us a view of what exactly we were dealing with.

"By the grace of Polimus...," Connor muttered in shock.

"I-I think I'm going to be- *BLEEEEGH*"

As Myrril lost her lunch behind me, I was staring into the burial room in front of us, processing the situation.

A little ways into the room we saw Smiles pinned to a heavy stone pillar with a spear through his chest. His torso quickly ended where his legs should have been. Instead, long pink tubes hung from underneath him, joining a pile of rancid smelling blood and guts on the ground below. His lower half was nowhere to be seen.

Just to the left, slumped against the wall, was another bloodied corpse. Its head and chest had been completely crushed into an unrecognizable paste, but judging by its gear I would say it was Lorenzo.

But for me, this gut-wrenching scene wasn't even the worst of it. Just beyond the fallen mercenaries were several humanoid shapes ready to charge.

"No..." I whispered.

These creatures had dry, mummified skin stretched across their frames. Their empty eye sockets stared into my soul, their mouths filled with rotted teeth.

My heart stopped, and time seemed nonexistent.

Flashes of scenes, memories started playing in my head.

I saw countless bodies rushing at me with grey skin and dead eyes. Their hands grasping and tearing my skin. I could feel my flesh being sundered, by bones broken, and my blood endlessly pouring.

"No..." I muttered once more, the light in my hands began to flicker.

Another flash of memory. Heads and hands of the dead reached from the darkness, digging into my eyes and ears and mouth. I was screaming, yet no sound came.

Eternity, that's what it felt like. An eternity of torment in but a moment.

"NO!" I screamed.

Before I knew it, I was back to reality with a spear in my hand. I unconsciously threw it with all my might, a blue tint coming over it as it flew through the air. The spear skewered the first Draugr and continued to fly, taking the creature with it as it pierced another and another before getting embedded in the wall.

The others had already rushed past me and into combat, my attack seemingly freezing the Draugr for just enough time.

It was irrational. I knew that Draugr were down here, I had seen them on the way down. The only difference was that these were moving.

"Elric!" Reginald yelled, "Snap out of it, we need help!"

His voice pierced my hazy mind and the world became clear once more. I looked and saw that they were barely holding their own.

I said nothing before I rushed into the fray. I jumped over the front line the others had made and drew my blade. With a few quick slashes, I removed the arms and head of a

Draugr who had underestimated me. The other Draugr, however, weren't going to make the same mistake.

Several of them locked their eyes on me and rushed. The first one swung a large sword different from the others. It was dark, but the guard was shaped like diamonds and the blade itself had runes carved down the fuller. I saw it coming, but for some reason I was unable to dodge in time. The blade struck me in my side, digging into my flesh about an inch before I was able to twist out of the way.

I kicked off of its chest and swung my blade at a Draugr behind me, cutting into its chest. As I landed, it turned back to me and raised a wicked looking morning star.

Instead of jumping backward, I dodge forward to get inside his range and stick my sword through its stomach. I had noticed before, but these creatures were a lot tougher than the Husks. It had to be due to their lineage.

As I grabbed my blade imbedded in its stomach, I twisted it sideways and pushed as I circled around, nearly bisecting it. I had trouble with its bones, noting that I needed to continue aiming for joints if I wanted to remove parts.

"Be careful! They may be dead, but they were once trained soldiers of the Aleurian Imperial Army!" I shouted to the others as the one I just attacked fell to the ground, unable to hold itself up.

I started to strike at the others around me, but they unfortunately started to learn my attack patterns, making it difficult to get in more than superficial hits. They, however, were able to get in plenty of strikes against me. I felt sharp pain and warm wetness from spots all around my body. I decided to retreat to the line so I can control where I'm being attacked from.

Connor was wielding his blade in his right hand, slashing away in a blur. After each strike, a bit of grey flesh flew into the air like he was carving a turkey at high speed. Edd looked like he was enjoying himself as he crushed ancient bone and smashed undead heads.

From behind, arrows and small bolts of fire rained over our heads. Arrows stuck out of various places in the Draugr and some where even catching on fire.

I caught a view of Reginald cutting into a Draugr before getting smacked in the shield with a mace.

My blade struck dried flesh once more as I jammed it through the open mouth of a Draugr.

As I did, a flash came once again. I saw the faces approaching from the darkness. My head began to pound, my chest got heavy, and I froze in place.

The light I had been holding went out, the battlefield only illuminated by some torches. Despite noticing, I couldn't move. Fear filled nearly every fiber of my being.

"Watch out!" I heard Connor yell, yet I was rooted to the spot.

In almost slow motion, I saw the first Draugr I fought approach and hold his weapon in a stance, a very familiar stance. It was the same one I had been taught in basic training. It was meant to cut through your enemy's defenses in one strike, ending the battle without wasting energy.

All I could do was watch as the blade slowly swung downward, then up again, cutting into me. I felt every painstaking movement of the blade as it traced a path from hip to shoulder, cutting through my armor, and splashing blood across the wall behind me.

Why can't I move! Come on body, just move!!

My knees buckled under me and my shirt became soaked and the edges of my vision became heavy.

"ELRIC!" I heard someone shouting.

I hit the ground on my knees and began to fall backward.

"*JUST! FUCKING! MOVE!*" I screamed internally.

"**REPENT**," A familiar voice echoed in my head.

A red light filled the space above me right before my vision faded away.

I was laying on the hard ground looking up at a sea of blue. White wisps gently floated across my vision.

"Elric," A stern but caring voice called out, "Get up. A soldier of the Aleurian Empire does not fall so easily."

I sat up and took in my surroundings. I was in a beautiful courtyard surrounded by beautiful flowers and with a large fountain in the center. Nearby was a beautiful building in the shape of a "U" made of white stone and carved with the utmost detail. The entire area was surrounded by a high wall with armored figures patrolling it regularly.

This familiar sight was Tors Manor, my home.

I looked down at myself. My hands were covered in welts and calluses, and a wooden sword sat on the ground next to me. My body looked much younger and bore very few of the scars I was used to seeing.

"Good, now stand and take up your arms," The voice called once more.

I obeyed, quickly standing and holding the wooden blade out in front of me.

Across the way was a tall man holding another wooden sword. His face was sharp and his blue eyes were filled with intelligence. He had dirty-blonde hair just like me and a well-trimmed goatee. He wore fine clothing that didn't even have a speck of dirt on it, and on his hand was a silver ring with the image of a wolf holding a hammer in its mouth.

"Yes, father," I said to him.

"Was that all a dream?" I wondered to myself.

"Now, come at me once more," My father commanded.

I rushed forward, shifting my weapon to give a powerful strike from below.

"Yaaaah!" I yelled as my blade swung forward.

My father quickly blocked, but my blade had already moved to strike from above. He had completely fallen for my feint.

Crack!

"What!?" I yelped in surprise.

My father's blade, which had been in the completely wrong place, had intercepted my strike and stopped it in its tracks.

"Hm. Better," My father said.

His heavy foot appeared from nowhere and struck my chest, sending me flying across the courtyard.

My father walked over to me, "If you were faster, that could have worked."

I nodded and got to my feet.

"Again," My father said.

"Father, before we go again, may I ask something?"

He nodded in response, "Of course, Elric."

"I feel that no matter how many times we spar, I can never get a hit in. How is it that you're so strong?" I asked.

My father gave a small grin, "I have something to protect, something I must not lose under any circumstance."

"But I have one!" I said enthusiastically, "I'm going to be a protector of the realm, just like you!"

My father chuckled, "That's a fine goal, but it's not what I mean."

"Then what do you mean?"

"When a warrior fights with nothing to protect, they will never achieve their true potential," Father explained, "So I'll ask you, do you have something you wish to protect?"

I turned my head to the side and smiled.

Father followed my gaze. There, poorly hiding behind a bush, was a small girl with golden hair and long, pointed ears.

"I see," My father turned back to me.

As I looked him in the eyes, I realized that we were the same height now. My body had returned to being covered in scars, and a long slash wound across my chest.

"A warrior who has nothing," My father started, "Will never surpass their limits in order to protect what they cannot afford to lose."

My eyes were locked with my fathers as a strange energy began to emanate from him. The sky went black and the wind whipped violently. My father's eyes began to change color.

"Make me proud, son."

Then, my eyes opened.

"ELRIC!" Myrril screamed after seeing her friend get cut.

She couldn't even see the creature's blade move. To her, one moment it was getting into a stance, then the next moment its blade was covered in blood and Elric had collapsed.

"Shit, this ain't good!" Shouted Connor, who had started to struggle with the Draugr in front of him.

"Connor, we need to regroup and come back with reinforcements," Carla calmy replied.

"N-No! We can't just leave Elric!" Myrril shouted furiously at Carla.

Myrril looked back to Elric and saw the Draugr moving in to finish him off. She pointed her staff towards it and closed her eyes, hoping to the Gods that she would make it in time.

She imagined the magical formula in her mind and willed the power within the air around her to obey.

"Please, just work!" She yelled in her mind.

A flash of light followed as power gathered at the Bloodstone at the tip of her staff.

"*Firebird!*"

Once the words left her mouth, the energy gathering in her staff burst forth towards the Draugr threatening Elric. It quickly formed into the shape of a burning eagle, soaring towards the undead creature.

"Gruh?" The Draugr let out a strange sound that seemed almost like confusion a moment before the firebird impacted.

Flame engulfed its form, lighting up the room. It let out a guttural cry through its rotten throat, desperately trying to pat the flames out.

"Nice going Myrril," Reginald shouted, "Can you do it again?"

Myrril dropped to her knees, breathing heavily. Sweat poured from her brow and she shook her head.

"Right," Reginald nodded, "Then we need to retreat. There's too many of them for us to take on in such an open place!"

"Agreed," Connor nodded.

"No!" Myrril shouted with a force that was unlike her, "We have to get Elric!"

"It's too dangerous," Reginald yelled, "I'm sorry but-"

Suddenly, a blue light filled the room. Myrril looked over and gasped.

"Elric!?"

Elric was standing where he had fallen, a bright blue light emanating from his eyes. Everyone, including the Draugr, froze and stared at him.

Then, flashes of purple started to overtake the blue, like bolts of lightning; and Elric muttered something in a language no-one there understood.

The air began to swirl around him in various pockets, condensing together and forming long, spear-like constructs of moving wind. Without warning, they shot forward at high speed.

They skewered the Draugr without fail, ending the threat in the blink of an eye. Once they were dead, the light faded from Elric's eyes, and he fell back to the ground, panting heavily.

"Elric! A-Are you all right?" Myrril was the first to break from her shock. She ran over to my side and helped me up.

"Yeah," I said while trying to catch my breath, "It's just a flesh wound."

"That was impressive," Reginald approached, holding out a waterskin, "I've never seen anyone cast that many spells at once."

I graciously accepted the waterskin and took a swig. My parched throat instantly felt better as the cool water washed against it.

"It takes practice," I said between drinks, "I was just lucky this time."

Connor walked up to us with a shocked look on his face.

"Woah. I thought ye were a swordsman," He started, "I never would 'ave guess ye were actually a Sorcerer!"

"That explains why you were able to do that so quickly, and without chanting a spell," Carla added.

"I'm actually a better swordsman than a magic user," I said whilst stretching.

"By the way, what happened?" Reginald asked, "It looked like you just froze."

I shook my head, "No, that Draugr was just much faster than me."

I decided to lie to them about what happened, it would be too much to explain and would also reveal my identity. Even then, I didn't want to burden them with my past.

"We're almost to the end," I changed the subject, "Only a few more rooms if I remember correctly."

"W-What!?" Myrril gasped, "Y-You're in n-no shape to c-continue!"

"Yeah, we need to get you out of here," Reginald agreed.

"No, I'm fine," I protested.

"Elric was so cool! Let him come with us, please!" Edd begged.

"We can't," Reginald said, "Look at that wound on his chest."

Connor looked at my chest and turned back to Reginald, "Looks like a scratch to me. Elric must have gotten really lucky."

"Wha!" Reginald exclaimed in surprise.

We went back and forth a few times, but I was finally able to convince Reginald and Myrril to let me continue after we rested for a few minutes.

Wow, everyone seems so concerned for my wellbeing. It's kind of weird.

After we rested, all six of us continued down the path. This time, Connor and Carla took the lead.

It was strange. When we were resting, the three from Lost Light split off and had a heated whispering argument that I wasn't able to hear, but ever since then they've been a little distant.

I was hoping they weren't acting weird because of me.

We came to a large, circular chamber with a high ceiling. In the center of the room was a sarcophagus surrounded by offering bowls and unlit candles.

"Is this it?" Reginald asked.

I shook my head, "No, this chamber is adjacent to the one we want."

"S-So we're almost d-done?" Myrril asked nervously.

"Yes, all we have left is a small hallway and then we're at the main burial chamber," I pointed at a set of stone doors at the other end of the room, "It's just through that door.

"Did you hear all of that?" I directed at Connor before I turned to see him and the other two huddling up once again.

"Hey, guys. We're ready to continue," I called out, "What's wrong?"

The three of them turned around to look at us and Connor began to speak.

"I'm truly sorry, Elric. But we're not goin any further."

I felt a little confused, wondering if this is why they were a little distant.

Then, I felt a searing pain in my lower back, and a warm wetness began to emanate from it.

I turned my head behind me and saw Carla standing there, holding a bloody knife. I looked at Connor, and sure enough Carla wasn't there anymore. I had never even seen her move.

"That is to say," Connor continued, a smile growing on his face, "None of ye will be goin any further."

CHAPTER 13

Treachery

Connor let out a crazed laugh, the smile on his face being accompanied by wild looking eyes. Edd stood next to him, a dumb grin on his face. Carla had also reappeared by his side.

"What?" I asked as I grabbed my wound.

Reginald ran up and blocked me with his shield, "What the hell is going on here Connor!?"

Connor chuckled, "What does it look like? We're stoppin all of ye from interrupting the necromancer."

"B-But why?" Myrril's voice sounded pained.

"It's obvious," I winced as I spoke, "They're working for him."

"Tsk, tsk," Connor waved his finger, "I wouldn't speak if I were ye. That dagger Carla stabbed ye with was coated in a potent poison."

Once he said it, I realized that it felt like something had entered by blood stream, a strange bit of pressure that shouldn't be there.

"And for the record," Connor continued, "We don't work for that lout, we were hired to help and protect him."

"So there are more people involved?" Reginald asked, his eyes locked with Connor's.

"Hmph. Even if we're about to kill ye, I'm not goin to spill all our secrets," Connor scoffed.

I was now on one knee, the pain shooting up my back was unbearable.

"So, what was the plan? You kill us once we made it deep enough in the tomb?" I asked.

"Hm, I suppose I can tell ye that," Connor sneered, "The original plan was for us to help ye to the necromancer and have him deal we ye, but you bein a sorcerer threw a wrench in the plan."

"Our backup was to have ye retreat once we saw the Draugr," Connor continued, "Which, by the way, we were just as surprised about as ye were."

I smiled, "I guess my stubbornness brought you to plan C then?"

"Aye, we didn't really want to fight ye ourselves," Connor replied, "Especially not after seein yer power, that's why we had to poison ye."

"Edd please!" Myrril called out, "Please tell me this isn't true!"

Edd looked at Myrril with remorse, "Sorry, Myrril. I liked you."

"N-No..." Myrril looked weak in the knees.

"Don't despair," I told her, "With the three of us, it'll be a walk in the park."

"Don't make me laugh," Connor said, "With ye in that condition, it won't be much of a challenge."

"What condition?" I asked.

"What!?" He shouted in surprise.

I rose to my feet and stared him down, "Poison this weak has no effect against me."

Treachery

"That's impossible!" His voice started to sound desperate, "That was enough poison to down a pack of bears!"

"Calm yourself," Carla said to him, "With that spell he did earlier, he must have expended most of his energy."

Connor took a deep breath, "You're right. We can still do this."

He unhooked his short sword from his left side, and reattached it to his right, drawing it with his left hand. At the same time, Carla took out two black daggers and Edd pulled out a massive, curved cleaver about four feet long.

"Carla, take the mage. I don't trust Edd to use his full strength against her," Connor commanded, "Edd, go play with the shield user. I'll take the sorcerer."

His companions nodded and stared down their prey.

"Elric, what should we do," Reginald whispered in a panic.

"It's okay, separate and take out the ones attacking you," I said, "They inadvertently split themselves into the best possible match up with us."

"A-Are you s-sure?" Myrril asked.

"Yes," I nodded, "Just do your best, and whoever finishes first go support whoever looks like they need it, if you still have strength left."

"Hm!" They both agreed with my plan and ran off to either side of the room, giving everyone ample room to move around.

Connor just smiled at me as we were left alone in the center of the room.

"Show me what you've got, Sorcerer."

As Myrril stood across from Carla she began to analyze the situation, desperately trying to figure out how she could possibly beat her.

"I am surprised," Carla said, narrowing her eyes.

"H-How so?" Myrril asked.

"You did not try to change his mind," She answered, "You simply went with his judgment. I am unable to tell if you trust him that much, or if you are just stupid."

Carla dropped into a stance, her blades held backwards in her grip.

"I-I guess we'll f-find out, *Fire Arrow!*"

A familiar bolt of flame shot from Myrril staff, but Carla moved to the side just in time to dodge.

"So we shall," Carla flipped one of her blades around and threw it.

Myrril instinctively pulled her arms closer to defend herself.

Thunk!

She couldn't believe it. The dagger that Carla had thrown was lodged in her staff. When she realized this, she looked back to Carla only to find her gone.

After seeing what had happened to Elric, Myrril jumped forward. A woosh sounded behind her as Carla's blade cut through the air.

Myrril spun around, her heart beating faster and faster, and unleashed more spells at Carla.

"*Fire Arrow! Fire Arrow!*"

The red light around the head of her staff glowed and

burst two more bolts forward. Both were easily dodged by Carla as she ran into Myrril's spell range.

"Ha!" Carla lunged at Myrril, who spun to the side just in time to reduce the attack to a glancing blow.

Myrril held one hand on the cut she received and used the other to swing her staff at Carla.

Carla ducked the staff and threw another blade into Myrril's unarmored body.

"AH!" Myrril cried in pain as the dagger dug into her shoulder.

She gritted her teeth and shouted, *"Fire Storm!"*

A wall of flame irrupted around her, forcing Carla to back away.

"If you were trying to kill me with that, you should reconsid-" Carla was cut off by more flaming arrows flying at her.

One managed to impact her arm, burning a hole through her clothing and blackening her skin.

"Tsk, I should have seen that coming," Carla sounded annoyed.

"I-I do know s-some basic t-tactics, you know," Myrril stuttered, the pain continuing to radiate from her shoulder and side.

Her opponent rushed forward once more, slashing at Myrril's arms, which she was unable to dodge in time.

Myrril almost dropped her staff, but managed to push through the pain and fire back at Carla.

Magical fire and black daggers flew back and forth, some reaching their targets while many more were dodged. Carla spent every moment she could taunting Myrril.

"Fire Arrow!"

"Your attacks are weak, just like your conviction."

"*Fire Arrow! Fire Arrow!*"

"Even if you can hit me a few lucky times, I've struck you many more."

Carla spoke the truth. Myrril was covered in small cuts and was slowly being covered in blood. Carla had taken several hits herself, but she wasn't looking nearly as bad as her opponent.

"Shut up!" Myrril yelled as sweat began to bead on her forehead.

Carla smiled, "If you cannot even take this, what will you do when other criticize you?"

Myrril started to shake, her fears bubbling up in her mind.

"*Fire Storm! Fire Arrow!*"

Carla moved out of the way of the screen Myrril had made.

"Ha! You cannot catch me by surprise again."

She rushed to the side then changed course to once again make a pass at Myrril.

Myrril hit one blade out of the air as Carla ran at her. Unable to recover from the wide movement, Myrril couldn't stop Carla from stabbing three times in Myrril's chest and back.

Myrril tumbled forward as Carla kept going. Her breathing became heavy and blood began to pool in her throat.

She weakly pointed her staff toward Carla and started to channel energy from the air. She imagined the spell she used earlier against the Draugr, and an intense red light began to emanate from the focus at the top of her staff.

"Fire Bird!"

The light shot from the staff toward Carla at an intense speed. Carla's eyes went wide, realizing she couldn't dodge it in time.

A moment later, the red firelight abruptly dissipated. Carla stood there, surprised. Then, she began to laugh.

"I knew it!" She said while letting out a deep chuckle, "When you cast that spell earlier, I knew it was just a fluke."

"N-No..." Myrril's voice was filled with despair.

The spell she cast had broken down before it reached the target. She knew the spell was beyond her abilities, but she had managed to cast it before and she was banking on being able to cast it again.

Carla suddenly appeared in front of Myrril and gave a heavy kick to her chest. Myrril was unable to brace in time and was sent backward a few feet, landing on her back.

Myrril groaned in pain as she tried to stand up, using her staff as a crutch.

"It is so funny," Carla continued to laugh, "I was so sure you were a danger to us, but you are just some fledgling mage!"

While listening to Carla, Myrril was racking her brain in an attempt to figure out a way to win. She knew this was life or death, and it wasn't only her life that relied on this battle.

She didn't want to kill Carla, she didn't want to kill anything. "However," she thought, "Maybe that's why I can't win?"

It made sense to her. This entire time she had been aiming to disable Carla, but her opponent wasn't so kind. Myrril knew that she had to kill Carla in order for her to survive, but her insecure nature was holding her back.

"*Do I even deserve to live?*" She asked herself.

She was never confident in her abilities. All her life, Myrril's older sister had been the outspoken prodigy while she was just the disappointment. She had once gained the confidence to foolishly challenge her sister, and promise to become the greatest mage in the world. Now, she was going to die like the failure she was.

Then, a voice called out to her.

"Myrril, don't freeze up!" It was Elric. He was trying to help her while in battle himself.

"We're counting on you to take care of Carla," he shouted once again, "You can do it!"

"You're counting on me?" Myrril whispered. Reginald was the only other person who had said that to her. It was the reason why she stuck with him. He saw her as a person instead of a failure.

Then, Myrril got an idea. It was an idea that even made her gain hope, not only in the situation but in herself.

"You still try to stand?" Carla asked as Myrril finally got to her feet, "I tried to make this easy on you, but oh well. I guess you like pain."

"*Fire Storm!*"

Carla jumped out of the way and began to sprint around to feint into Myrril again, but she was met by another wall of flame.

Myrril was firing off Fire Storm everywhere Carla went, creating a wall of flame that singed her opponent.

Then, flaming bolts flew from beyond the walls of fire, directed at Carla. However, Carla had already seen this trick twice before and was prepared for it.

Treachery

"I knew it. You are just a two-spell phony!" Carla taunted once more.

She used her incredible speed to make Myrril cast another spell, then she doubled back and curved around the wall of flame. Myrril's back was to her, light gathered at her staff as she prepared to cast another spell.

Carla rushed toward Myrril's back.

"It's time to say goodbye!" She yelled as she plunged her daggers down at Myrril's neck.

"You're right, it is time to say goodbye."

"Huh?"

Carla felt something impact her stomach as she was partially held in the air by Myrril's staff. She had spun at thrust it at Carla after she had fallen into the trap Myrril had devised.

"Though, you were also wrong," Myrril said, completely devoid of uncertainty, "I'm a three-spell phony. *Flameburst!*"

Thump! Thump! Thump!

Carla's face was filled with surprise as a powerful force pushed against her mid-section in three dull thumps.

The burst of flame pushed through Carla's flesh and punched a hole clean through her stomach and out her back. Seared flesh was thrown through the air, and Carla went limp on the end of Myrril's staff.

Reginald and Edd rushed at each other as soon as they moved away from the others. The sound of metal on metal resounded as their blades clashed.

Reginald was taking more of a defensive approach,

blocking or parrying strikes when he could, and attacking in Edd's blind spots. Edd, on the other hand, was attacking viciously and without remorse; a child-like smile plastered on his face.

"This is fun!" Edd shouted with glee as he swung his curved cleaver at Reginald's head.

Reginald ducked and jumped to the side, swinging his blade at Edd's open side. It was quickly parried by a massive fist, which then pushed its way into Reginald's shield.

"How is this fun!?" Reginald shouted with panic.

Edd's cleaver scraped across the kite shield, pushing Reginald back a few inches.

"More, More!" Edd jumped up and down, an image of pure joy on his face.

"This isn't a game!" Reginald shouted as he dodged another swing.

Reginald was getting frustrated at how Edd was acting, but he was even more frustrated by just how strong he was.

"How the hell is he putting this much power into his strikes?" He thought to himself, *"I guess it's a good thing he thinks it's a game, I would have a big problem if he was completely serious."*

Reginald continued to evade Edd's attacks as he waited for an opening. At one point, Edd swung a little too hard and was slightly off balance. Reginald wasted no time taking advantage of the opening.

He grabbed his blade tightly and thrust it into Edd's stomach where it made a horrific *Squelch* as it bit into the soft flesh.

"Owie!" Edd cried as Reginald pulled his blade back and stepped away from his opponent.

Edd grabbed his stomach, continuing to shout about the pain.

"It huuuurts! Ow, ow, ow!"

In any other situation, Reginald would have found it amusing to see a grown man act this way, amusing and slightly disturbing. However, this wasn't any other situation, this was a fight to the death and one that just got deadlier.

Edd was now wildly flailing his weapon as he cried out in pain.

Reginald realized it then that Edd had the mind of a child. The way he acted and spoke lent to this realization. It made Reginald pause for a moment and wonder if they really had to kill him. He believed that Edd had been tricked into doing horrible things, thinking that it was just a game.

That moment Reginald took was a mistake.

In the time it took to blink, Edd's blade had impacted with Reginald, sending him flying to the side. Luckily, Reginald was hit with the flat of the blade, so his wounds were minor.

He shakily got to his feet, "Oh, Gods. That wasn't good," He mused to himself.

Then, Edd appeared in front of him, seemingly no longer throwing a tantrum.

"You gave me an Owie," Edd said to Reginald, pure menace radiating from him as he spoke, "Now I'm gonna give you an Owie."

A shiver ran through Reginald's spine as every fiber of his being told him to run, but he was stuck where he stood. The pure amount of death radiating from Edd was enough to make him freeze where he stood.

Then, a voice reached his ears, "...don't freeze up!"

Reginald recognized it as Elric, and his tunnel vision dissipated. He jumped back, narrowly dodging Edd's blade which came down from above. Reginald took that moment to slash into Edd's skin several more times, blood splashing across both of them.

Then, another sound echoed through the chamber.

Thump! Thump! Thump!

From the corner of his eye, Reginald saw a ball of fire burst from Carla's back, and the image of a bloodied Myrril standing in front of her.

Reginald couldn't help but smile, "I knew she could do it."

Edd, on the other hand, wasn't in such a good mood.

"Carla! RAAAAAAAAAAAH!"

He screamed madly at the sight of his friend's corpse, the veins in his neck and arms bulging.

"I HATE YOU!" Edd yelled into the air before locking eyes with Reginald. They were no longer the child-like eyes he had before, these were bloodshot and filled with rage.

His blade came from nowhere, leaving Reginald no time to move his shield. Instead, he moved his blade in an effort to parry Edd's weapon once more.

SNAP!

Reginald's weapon couldn't take the force of the impact, sending the top half flying through the air. As he was taking in this information, Edd's off hand struck like a snake, and grabbed Reginald by the throat.

"I hate you!" Edd repeated as he squeezed his clenched fist.

Reginald began kicking wildly as his neck was slowly being crushed. His efforts to pull Edd's massive fist apart was to no avail, and even stabbing Edd with his broken broadsword did nothing to dissuade him.

Finally, just as Reginald's face started to turn blue, his leg reached a critical area.

"AGH!" Edd screamed in pain as Reginald's steel boot impacted his family jewels. He looked at Reginald in his hand with even more disdain than before, pulling his arm back and throwing Reginald across the room.

As he gasped for breath in the air, Reginald met no relief. Edd appeared ahead of him and threw a massive fist into Reginald's head. The impact rattled his brain and he was slammed into the hard stone floor.

A shadow appeared from above Reginald, "Just go away!"

Gasping for breath through a crushed windpipe, Reginald got to his knees and held his shield up. A moment later, a flurry of blows impacted the kite shield as Edd furiously pummeled it with his cleaver.

"D...amn," Reginald croaked.

He began to look for a way out as his breathing steadied a bit. His shield had started to groan under the strain and cracks appeared in its surface.

Reginald only saw one opening. He waited as long as he could, until he was sure his shield couldn't take another hit, and rolled to the side as Edd's weapon sunk into the ground where Reginald was just kneeling.

"Why won't you just go away!?" The way Edd spoke sounded like he was pouting. He tried to pull his blade from the stone floor, but it was lodged rather firmly.

"I... can't just leave... my friends," Reginald managed to painfully say.

He tightened his grip on the broken sword and held his shield in front of him, charging straight for the massive man.

"I don't want to play with you anymore!"

Edd swung his fist directly into Reginald's shield, sending metal shards and wooden splinters flying in all directions.

Reginald took the moment before impact to hit the ground, sacrificing his shield to slide between Edd's legs. He pushed himself up as he slid before kicking off the ground at an angle, pushing his fatigued legs past their limit to fire himself back at Edd. He twisted himself the best he could in midair towards his target, and grasped his broken weapon with both hands as he plunged it into Edd's shoulder.

"GAAAAAUUUH!" Edd screamed in pain as he flailed wildly, trying to grab at Reginald, but his massive muscles made it difficult to reach behind him.

Reginald planted his feet on Edd's back and pulled his blade diagonally with all his might in an attempt to copy a move he had seen Elric pull off.

Edd screamed even more as the blade tore through his flesh.

Reginald knew he wouldn't be able to cut through bone with just his legs, so he pushed off of Edd's back and used the weight of his body to pull his sword further down.

There was a loud crack as Edd's spine shattered, the jolt shaking Reginald loose.

Edd's legs faltered as his scream suddenly became silent.

Reginald ducked out of the way as his opponent spun around and slammed face first into the ground, unmoving.

Reginald was breathing heavily, his whole body was sore and his throat throbbed with pain.

Treachery

He looked down at his broken sword and sighed, "I won't... be much use... like this."

He looked up at the fight going on between Elric and Connor with a smile.

"Not that... it looks like... he needs help."

I drew my blade and stared at Connor, who was standing across from me holding his own weapon. All we did was lock eyes and stare, neither wanting to make the first move.

The battles to either side had already begun, and I was able to keep track of what was going on using my peripheral vision.

Then, without warning, Connor shifted his back leg. He pushed off the ground and sprinted at me faster than I had expected.

Clang!

Our blades met between us, our eyes locked the whole time.

I pushed him back with my blade and swung again. I was met with his blade this time, stopping mine in its tracks.

Back and forth we went, again and again; Our blades connecting each time we swung despite the rhythm slowly increasing with each strike.

We began to circle each other, keeping a wide area between us.

Connor smiled, "I wasn't expecting ye to also be Etterkommer."

"Etterkommer?" I asked, keeping my guard up.

We exchanged a few more blows before he answered.

"So ye don't know? Let me enlighten ye," Connor responded before rushing in for another strike.

"Etterkommer are those of us with the blood of Aleurians runnin through us," He explained whilst holding his blade against mine.

"Is that so?" I jumped back, then rushed forward again.

"Aye," Connor said while casually intercepting by blade, "We 'ave more power than other humans, meanin we're superior. It explains why yer able to be a Sorcerer."

We exchanged more blows while he spoke, "We don't 'ave to fight. Ye can join me, and rule over the peons of this world."

"You believe you're better than everyone else?" I asked.

"Of course! I 'ave more power than anyone. I'm stronger, smarter, I am superior in every way!" Connor responded with passion.

I hopped away and pointed my blade toward him.

"You're wrong," I said, "Even if you have a superior body and mind than someone, it doesn't mean you're better than them. It certainly doesn't mean you can underestimate them."

When I was much younger, I looked down on the other races because they weren't Aleurian. My father was the one who taught me that just because we were born into a superior race, it doesn't mean we are better than everyone. Strength and Intelligence doesn't correlate to being right.

"I suppose it was a lot to ask," Connor sighed, then looked back at me, "Now, then. Shall we dispense with the warm-up?"

I nodded, and launched myself at great speed toward my opponent.

Treachery

With our probing attacks over, I decided to put a decent amount of power into my attack, somewhere at the peak of human physicality. However...

Clank!

Connor deflected my attack and stabbed forward with his short sword. I had a longer reach, but he was able to strike within my guard if he got close enough.

I twisted my body to try and evade, but I still felt a sharp pain on the side of my chest. It's an area that would have been covered by armor if it hadn't been completely destroyed by that Draugr from earlier.

"Yer fast, but not fast enough," Connor told me as he struck again and again.

His blade grazed me several times, but I was able to dodge them for the most part.

Then, I jumped back while swinging my blade down in order to create space between us. It was successful, and Connor jumped back as well to avoid taking a hit.

"Who do you work for?" I asked as I rushed back at Connor. He leapt over me and struck at my back, but I twisted in time to knock is blade away. Unfortunately, I couldn't strike back without risking being on the ground, so I regained my balance instead.

"Like I said before, I'm not sayin a thing," He stabbed towards me and I parried it away, hitting him in the face with the butt of my sword, "Urg!"

"I'm not taking no for an answer," I said as Connor stumbled back, holding his nose.

"It seems ye 'ave some trainin," He wiped away blood coming from his nose, "But I still ain't talkin."

We rushed at each other again, our movements looking

more like a dance than a fight. However, I was steadily losing. My arms and torso were covered in cuts, and my chest wound from earlier had reopened.

Then, I heard a bit of laughter in the air.

Out of the corner of my eye, I caught Myrril struggling to get to her feet while Carla stood nearby letting out a cry of amusement. Myrril looked conflicted, it was a look I had seen many times in soldiers. It ended in one of two ways, either they killed their foe, or they themselves were killed.

"Myrril, don't freeze up!" I shouted towards her, "We're counting on you to take care of Carla. You can do it!"

A blade came from nowhere, causing me to duck.

"Don't get distracted, or ye might lose yer head," Connor smiled devilishly.

As I ducked, I lunged up and managed to inflict a wound across his shoulder.

"Erk, lucky hit."

Connor backed off with a wry smile on his face. I didn't waste this moment and pushed my attack, sending Connor into a defensive position.

Thump! Thump! Thump!

"Carla! Damn," Connor sounded frustrated as we both caught a glimpse of Myrril's success.

"Now who's getting distracted?" I asked as I brought my sword down.

He deflected my attack and stabbed at me with his own. I twisted out of the way and used the momentum to land a hard kick at Connor's head. He quickly recovered from the daze and struck at me again, even faster this time. Sweat began to form on his forehead, and I could sense magical energy beginning to run through his body. He was using a form of body enhancement to increase his speed and strength.

My normal sight was struggling to keep up, so I used my own form of body enhancement. I willed the Megin within my body to flow into my eyes. Once it took effect, I no longer had trouble keeping up with Connor.

As we clashed blades once more, Connor held my sword in place with his own and threw a punch with his off hand. I grabbed his fist with my own free hand and gave Connor a good headbutt.

I was slowly gaining ground on him as more of my attacks connected. They were only light cuts, but it was better than nothing. As time went on, he showed more and more signs of fatigue, though I suppose I was as well.

Both of us were breathing heavily as our bodies craved more air and our muscles ached. My throat was dry as a bone, and my legs felt like lead, but I pushed on. To slow then was to accept death.

"Damn, yer better than I thought," Connor sneered.

"So are you," I replied.

I flipped back as his blade came for my heart, pushing off the ground once I landed. Connor blocked my strike and kicked at me, which I intercepted with my knee. I responded by elbowing him in the face, and taking a strike to the arm.

Warm blood had covered my left arm and torso, but it was nothing to me.

My blade flew once more at Connor's face. He hurriedly swung his blade and swatted mine out of the way, but only enough to avoid a fatal hit. I still connected with flesh, carving a path through his cheek and ear.

Connor's fist impacted my stomach, knocking the wind

out of me and his elbow came down on my back. I leapt back as I gasped for breath, instinctively bringing my sword into a defensive position as metal on metal resounded through the space.

I retreated a few paces to catch my breath before heading back into the fray, but Connor didn't let up.

"GAAAAAUUUH!" A pained scream echoed through the chamber as we saw Edd fall to the ground, unmoving.

"Edd, too?" Connor sounded surprised and disappointed, "I suppose I'll 'ave to do this myself."

More energy began to course through Connor as he poured more Megin into his body.

"I'll take care of ye, then yer friends."

He struck at me, taunting me as he did it. His attacks had gotten even faster and I was unable to keep up once again. I did my best to protect myself, but it was futile.

Connor unleashed a series of attacks with his sword, fist, and legs. I was pummeled and cut across my whole body. Blood poured from my head and into my eyes.

With one final kick I was sent into the wall, dazed and exhausted.

Connor began to laugh as he stood over me, "Do ye understand now? I am the strongest being alive! The power of the Aleurians flows through me!"

He began to ramble as I tried to catch my breath.

"With this power, I can rule the entire continent; nay, the entire world! Nobody'll be able to stop me. Not kings or emperors, not knights or armies, and especially not mercenaries."

He looked down at me, bloody and battered against the wall, "Ye could 'ave been privy to this power, if only ye

Treachery

had joined me when I offered. It's too late now, even if ye beg."

He stared at the roof and laughed, "It feels so good to kill another Etterkommer. If this is how powerful I am, I wonder just how powerful the Aleurians really were."

"Th..." I tried to speak, but I was getting lightheaded.

"I'm sorry, what was that?" Connor looked down at me and jammed his foot into my stomach, smiling once more, "It's funny that ye would even think to- What!?"

His smile faded as he noticed me staring into his eyes, the blood no longer flowing from my wounds. In fact, he had probably been surprised because he saw those very wounds closing before his eyes.

"If you want to know how powerful the Aleurians were," I got to my feet as Connor slowly backed away, his face twisted in fear, "Then why don't I show you?"

I decided to stop holding back against him and exercise my full power. Energy began to course through my veins and strengthen my body. While Connor had expended Megin to strengthen himself, I was circulating it through my body and letting it flow freely like a river instead of trying to force it. This was the true way to use Body Enhancement, the original way.

My arm moved faster than it had in a long time, bringing my blade along with it.

CLANG

Connor barely blocked my strike with his sword.

"Th-That wasn't so fast," He stuttered.

"Maybe," I said, locking eyes with him, "But I'll let you in on a little secret."

"Huh?"

I leaned in a little bit and whispered, "The longsword isn't what I specialize in."

Fear began to spread across Connor's face as his eyes moved wildly, trying to find a way out, but it was too late.

I twisted my sword around into a reverse grip, using it to push Connors's blade to the side. At the same time, emerging from a swirling vortex next to me was a beautifully engraved cup hilt. I used my free hand to grasp the hilt and pull it from the vortex to reveal a long, thin blade engraved with the same designs that graced my longsword.

Without wasting a moment, I quickly thrust the rapier three times into Connor's stomach.

He stumbled backward, clutching his fresh wounds and glaring at me, "Wha... HOW!?"

I took a step forward, he took a step back. Then, he seemed to steel himself and tighten his grip on his sword.

"I-It doesn't matter, I'm the strongest in the world! Yer just a weak sorcerer!" He screamed as he rushed forward.

Unfortunately for him, I was serious. Each time he attacked, I redirected his blade with my longsword and struck his torso several times with my rapier. Holes began appearing all over his body, each one gushing a massive amount of blood.

"WHY. CAN'T. I. Kill. YE!" He screamed as he attacked wildly, "I'm the strongest in the- Blugh."

Connor coughed up blood mid-sentence. It was to be expected, I had made a pincushion out of his lungs.

Eventually, Connor's weapon fell out of his hand and clattered on the floor as he dropped to his knees.

"...How?" Blood still poured from his mouth.

I shook the blood off my longsword and returned it to its

Treachery

scabbard before stabbing my rapier through his throat. Blood gurgled in his throat as he tried to speak.

"It's simple," I grabbed the blade of my rapier with my free hand and leaned down to Connor's ear, "You messed with the real thing."

A slight light of understanding shined in Connor's eyes before I pushed one arm forward and pulled with the other. A sickening *Crack* could be heard as I twisted his neck in an unnatural way; the life leaving his eyes.

I cleaned the blood from my weapon and returned it to storage in my pocket dimension. I looked down at the corpse of Connor O'Donner and sighed. I had some respect for him, sticking to his beliefs until the end.

"Hey! You guys still alive?" I called out.

"S-Somehow..." Myrril responded, a little shaky. She was on the ground, leaning against the wall on the other side of the room.

I looked next to the body of Edd and saw Reginald sprawled across the floor, giving a thumbs up.

"Good," I gave a sigh of relief, "How about we take five?"

Reginald raised his head to look at me, "Sounds good," Then he dropped it back down.

"Sure..." Myrril replied, staring lifelessly into the air.

Both of their voices were completely monotone like they had emotionally checked out for the day. I really couldn't blame them though, I was feeling the same way.

As soon as I sat on the ground, fatigue took over.

"Maybe we'll take ten..."

CHAPTER 14

Lord of Edren

Lords Burial Chamber – Tomb of the Fallen, Edren.

Kane stood in the center of the room, wiping sweat from his brow. He quickly turned to the robed figure nearby, "The ritual is ready, gather everyone."

"Yes sir, at once."

The figure bowed and rushed away to gather several other robed figures, who organized themselves in a circle around the center of the room. Each one stood on part of a massive magical equation written on the ground, a Magic Circle.

"Let us begin," Kane stated, causing everyone to raise their arms forward and begin chanting.

Kane was initiating a massive ritual that required an immense amount of magic, more than any single person could channel.

As he joined in, the circle began to glow a deep burgundy-purple. Megin started to flow from the air and into the sarcophagus at the center of the circle.

Suddenly, a massive crash echoed through the chamber.
BAAANNNG!

The stone doors flew open, slamming against the wall.

Three figures rushed forward, the one in the front shouting with a strange accent.

"Halt, Necromancer! Surrender and no harm shall befall you."

After we had rested for a few minutes, we rushed down the hallway connecting the two chambers, and I kicked the door open.

We stood in a massive chamber filled with treasures of all kinds, and decorated to be fit for a King. In the center, a group of robed people stood around a sarcophagus, chanting and sending magical energy into it.

I stood in front, with Myrril and Reginald behind me. Reginald now held a round shield he had taken from a corpse, and Connor's short sword.

As soon as we burst through the doors, I pointed my blade at the group of people and shouted a warning.

"Halt, Necromancer! Surrender and no harm shall befall you."

The figure with his hood down turned to look at me. My gaze was greeted by an intelligent looking man with slick black hair and round glasses.

"Those damn mercs. They aren't good for anything. Why couldn't they have sent me better help..." The man mumbled.

He looked back at us and began to speak, "Greetings, whoever you are. Thank you for the opportunity to surrender. However, I, the great Kane Ovid, cannot accept."

Why did he just give his name away that easily. Is everyone I fight going to be some egotistical maniac?

A smile creeped across Kane's face, "You see, I have been given the task of purging this puny city so that we may use it. I cannot simply stop."

Reginald stepped forward, "You would rather lose your life than abandon your duty?"

Kane began to chuckle, "Oh, you silly boy. My duty is more important than you can fathom. Taking this city is only the first step. Our ideals cannot be contained by a single city, nor a single country. We are the embodiment of the world's ideals, its desires."

He sighed, "That being said, I have no intention of dying here."

"Does that mean you surrender?" I asked hopefully.

"Oh, you stupid child. I plan on doing no such thing," Kane arrogantly said, "Instead, you will give my new friend here a warmup."

The light coming from the ground suddenly vanished.

"Ugh," A voice came from the center of the room, the sarcophagus.

That's impossible!

The corpse, or the previous corpse, sat up from its laying position and stretched its neck.

"It feels as though I have been asleep for a millennia," The voice that came from it was masculine, a voice that tickled the back of my mind.

The man had dark hair, combed to the side. His face was well-shaped and handsome, despite his skin being a light gray color. I felt a massive amount of Megin coming from him. The feeling of it was familiar...

"That's because you have, Lord Arthur," Kane said to the man.

The man, Arthur, stood in his sarcophagus and with a small leap, lightly floated to the ground next to Kane.

"I see," He said, "That would explain the poor state of this place."

Then, something clicked in my mind.

"No way," I said aloud.

Reginald looked at me, "What is it?"

"That's Arthur Edgar Tors," I explained in disbelief, "He was the Lord of Edren during the civil war. His father was Wolfram, the one man army."

"What?" Reginald shouted in surprise, "Do you mean to say the necromancer created a powerful undead warrior?"

I shook my head, "No. Arthur was a great mage."

Myrril's face went white, "S-So it's a lich?"

I nodded, "Unfortunately."

A Lich was a type of powerful undead spellcaster. They had the usual traits of the undead, except they kept their mind. Their memories and personalities remained intact, and since they were kept alive by the forces of Megin, their attack abilities were supposedly off the charts.

As far as I knew, they only occurred naturally, and very rarely at that. A rate that could easily confine them to legend. However, with the invention of Necromancy, I had no real basis anymore.

"If you don't mind, Arthur," Kane spoke to him as if they were best friends, "Could you take care of those pests for me?"

"Hm. I suppose I could take care of that."

He started to float towards us as the necromancer and his

followers began to run towards a corner of the room. There, I could see a dark tunnel that seemed to have been dug. It probably led out of the Tomb.

Suddenly, Arthur stopped in his tracks and tilted his head.

"Elric? Is that truly you?" He asked as we looked each other in the eye.

I gritted my teeth, "Hello, uncle."

A smile grew across his face, "Aha! So my eyes have not deceived me. How is it that you are here? A millennia has passed, no? ...Now that I say it aloud, that is quite strange, yes." He started to trail off into thought at the end.

As for me, I was a whirlwind of emotion. However, I steeled myself and suppressed them, facing the unnatural being my uncle had been turned to.

"Hey, what do you mean by uncle?" Reginald whispered in my ear.

I Ignored his question and gave an order instead, "You and Myrril need to stop the Necromancer and his followers from escaping. Try to capture as many as you can."

"But..."

"Just do it," I said forcefully.

They briefly looked to each other in confusion before chasing after the fleeing enemies.

Arthur paid them no attention, his focus was completely on me.

I looked back at my uncle and responded in the tongue of our people, "He tells the truth. It's been over eleven hundred years. The Aleurian Empire has fallen."

He nodded, and responded in kind, "I expected as much. My memories of my final moments are hazy, however, it appears I was done in my one of our own. Hm... I cannot seem to recall who it was."

He put a hand to his temple, trying desperately to remember.

"Uncle," I called out, "You've been raised from the dead by a magic called Necromancy. The humans invented it."

"Ah, that would be the reason for this strange feeling," My uncle looked at his own hands front and back. I got the sense that his memories and logic were a little fuzzy.

Then, he looked up at me, "Ah, yes. I suppose I was ordered to stop you."

"I'm sorry uncle, but could you please stand down?" I asked hopefully.

"Hm," He looked up in thought, "It appears that this 'Necromancy' you spoke of has some sort of mind-altering effect. My mental faculties remain, as do my memories. I recognize you as my nephew, Elric. However, there appears to be another feeling within me, akin to an instinct. It is telling me to obey Kane, and it is quite forceful."

Energy began to gather in Uncle Arthur's hands.

"I apologize, Elric. But it seems you will have to die."

I remember seeing my uncle fight in a tournament before. Seeing him floating around the ring, firing off blasts of magic at his adversary was a sight to behold. However, now that I was experiencing it firsthand, I finally knew the fear his opponents must have.

The chamber seemed to dim for a moment as a beam of light, colored like the rays of the sun, shot from his hand; aimed toward my head. I panicked and lost my balance, thankfully tumbling backward below the ray of light. Behind me, I could see a circular indent where the stone had become singed.

"Hm, it seems as though my capabilities are somewhat limited. Perhaps a large portion of my power is being used to maintain my form..." My uncle mused as I regained my footing.

The chamber dimmed once more as another beam of light shot toward me with great speed, but this time I didn't run. I held my arm up and willed my internal energy to form a barrier in front of my palm. A translucent force rippled outward from my palm and formed a barrier, dissipating the beam upon contact.

"So, you've learned how to block magic attacks, good," My uncle sounded genuinely happy despite trying to kill me.

The magic I used to block his attack was a technique taught to Aleurian soldiers who specialize in light combat and don't carry a shield with them. I wasn't one of those soldiers, but my father had taught me this technique anyway.

I ducked a blade of wind flying through the air and rushed toward my attacker. I swung and managed to land a cut on his side as he tried to dodge. It seemed that his reaction times were slower than usual.

"I see you still have the sword your father gave you. Do you still have the others as well?" Uncle Arthur chatted like it was a family reunion.

"Yeah," I said as I dodged another magic attack, "I even used them recently."

The weapons we were referring to were my Longsword, Rapier, and Spear; all of which were a set given to me by my father when I finished basic training.

"Good. Your father would be proud."

A ball of flame exploded in front of me, the force sending me backward.

I used my motion to spin in the air and land my feet on the wall, kicking off and flying through the smoke toward my uncle. I held my blade to the side and spun my torso to give me more force in midair.

My uncle didn't seem to be expecting it and took the hit across the chest. Black ichor began to seep from the wound.

"Huh, that was unexpected," He touched the ichor and looked at it on his fingers, "It seems I truly am dead."

I skidded to a halt behind him and pushed off once more. However, I was smacked by a pillar of solid rock as it emerged from the ground.

"Augh!" I had the wind knocked out of me, but I couldn't just freeze In place. I rolled sideways as a barrage of icicles fell onto me. I took several hits, but it wasn't nearly as bad as it would have been if I hadn't moved.

"You are decent at fighting, but your movements are too predictable," Uncle said as if lecturing a trainee, "Try mixing it up a bit, and use some magic."

I got to my feet and readied my blade for another strike, just as icicles rained upon me again. I conjured another barrier in time, but left myself open to another attack.

A beam of light hit my stomach and emerged out the back. The wound itself was seared, and no blood poured from it, but the pain was excruciating.

"You also leave too many openings. Do not simply stand still; dodge and attack at the same time."

I grit my teeth in pain and said, "Easier said than done."

I ducked to the side as another beam headed for me and used my barrier to reduce the impact of another explosion.

Dust rained from the ceiling and stone debris on the ground shook. I was concerned that the room wasn't stable enough to be throwing explosions around, but apparently, my uncle didn't agree.

Stone rods, similar to stalagmites, fired at me from the side. I was able to cut one in half and dodge another, but a third struck my thigh and stuck out the other side.

I cried out in pain, but I knew I had no time to stand around. My mind was hazy, but I attempted to move anyway. The pain around my leg grew immensely as my muscles tore and blood poured from around the stone rod.

"Have you been practicing every day?" Uncle asked accusingly.

My leg was like a searing pan, but I pushed through and rolled away from another barrage of ice.

"Uncle, stop this!" I shouted, "Don't let some weak magic control you!"

Two more beams fired at me and I had no way to dodge. I took one in the shoulder and one in the arm.

"It appears this magic is stronger than you thought," Uncle explained, "I won't be able to disobey. I truly am sorry."

I took a deep breath and attempted to calm myself to prevent a panic attack. I focused my mind on the situation at hand and locked away my emotions. If I was to survive this, there wasn't time for sentiment.

Megin poured through my body, strengthening every bone and muscle even further than when I fought Connor.

I opened my eyes and grabbed the stone rod embedded

in my leg. I pulled with all my might and tore it free. My mind became dark for a moment as pain was the only sensation I was able to feel.

Shakily, I got to my feet and directed more Megin to my wounds. Within a moment, they began to close themselves.

Aleurians had higher natural healing than humans did, but I was born with an even higher one. This, coupled with the self-healing technique my father taught me, was able to heal large wounds faster than normal magic.

Uncle Arthur smiled, "I see you are even faster at healing than I remember."

"I've learned a lot in the last few years," I replied without emotion.

"Then show me."

I ran at him with heightened speed. I moved out of the way of another stone pillar and a combination of icicles and fire shards, weaving past all of them to arrive at my Uncle.

He put up a barrier of his own, which my sword scraped off of, and I continued past him. I knew that if you were proficient enough at creating a barrier from Megin it could even block physical attacks, but I had never seen it myself.

As I spun, my spear appeared in my hand, and the next second it was cutting through the air on a warpath.

My uncle swatted the spear out of the way but completely missed my appearance. With rapier in hand, I stabbed into his back and sliced his arms. A fist flew from the side and impacted me with immense force. He must have imbued his fist with Megin, a very useful close-range technique for a long-range spellcaster.

I took another deep breath and rushed directly to his front. There, I saw what I was looking for.

Energy began to gather in his palms for two more energy beams. I poured more Megin into my body, pushing it past its limits for just a second so I could make it. I approached faster than he could set his spell off and stabbed a blade into either forearm. I changed my grips to hold them in reverse and pushed as hard as I could. My uncle's arms violently snapped and moved his palms to point at his chest.

A flash of light went off, and a large hole appeared in his chest. I removed my blades and jumped back to get some distance.

My uncle's arms fell limply to the side, the bones in his forearm completely shattered.

He smiled, "That was good, using my reduced reaction time to force my attack to hit myself."

Thump.

He fell backward, hitting the ground hard.

"Uncle!" I rushed toward him as I felt his energy fading.

"Elric, you've grown," he said weakly, "I'm sorry I wasn't able to resist the command."

"It's okay," I told him, "I know you were holding back."

He smiled, "My command was to kill you. It didn't specify how."

As I looked down at him, I felt a sense of piercing sadness. Though, it somehow felt far away.

"Elric," Uncle Arthur's face became serious, "I've always thought of you like my own son, so I must leave something with you."

I nodded as I tried to understand what I was feeling, "Anything."

"I need you to watch over Edren for me," His voice was getting weaker and his eyes began to close.

"Of course, uncle. I won't let anything happen to your people."

A light smile appeared on his face, "Thank you... Elric..."

As the last moments of my uncle's second life came to an end, I felt at that moment a disturbance in my soul. Like a piece of glass creaking as a crack grows inside, the sound echoed in my mind for but a moment, but my mind was in no state to process it.

I carefully lifted my uncle into my arms and carried him back to his sarcophagus, gently placing him back to rest.

"Goodbye, uncle," I whispered.

Then, I heard a sound and whipped my head toward the source.

Standing near the tunnel were Reginald and Myrril carrying three unconscious figures.

I quickly gathered my thoughts before calling out to them, "It's over."

"The Necromancer escaped, but we were able to capture these three," Reginald said.

I nodded in acknowledgment.

Myrril and Reginald looked at each other, then back at me. It seemed as though they wanted to say something, but instead just stood there in silence.

EPILOGUE

When Sean and the others arrived, I left Reginald and Myrril to explain the situation while I went back to the inn. I was almost stopped several times on the way out of the tomb, but the mercs were smart enough to know the mood I was in.

I trudged my way through the muddy streets and as soon as I got back to my room, I collapsed on the bed. Knowing someone is dead was much different from seeing it for yourself. You felt pain and sadness, but you were mostly able to keep it together until you saw for yourself.

However, what concerned me was how I felt at that moment. I still felt the loss, but the emotional torrent I expected never came. It felt like my emotions were stuck behind a bubble.

There was a knock on my door who knows how long later, but I ignored it.

Eventually, my exhaustion overtook me, and I fell asleep to the sound of rain pattering against the window.

My dreams were assaulted by horrible images of the dead. They chased me through a field of fire and ice. When they caught me, they tore at my flesh and dragged me back. Then, it was all dark. Heads and hands appeared from the emptiness and tore at my face.

Epilogue

It was the same dream I saw after we fought the Husks, but this time it was more vivid. Even more than what I saw while fighting the Draugr.

I had been having this dream off and on since I first woke in Kyrtvale, and just like every other time, I woke in the middle of the night drenched in cold sweat.

When morning came, I stayed in bed. Throughout the day, there were several knocks on the door, but I ignored all of them.

Every night I had the same nightmare, and every night I woke in a cold sweat. During the day I ignored knocks on the door and lay in bed staring at the ceiling.

Finally, at the end of the week, I left my room.

"Hey, Are you okay?" Fredrich asked, his voice filled with concern.

"Yeah, I'm fine."

I handed him some more money and left the Inn. I didn't have any goal in mind, I just wanted to wander.

I took in the sights of the inner district, trying to remember what it used to look like.

Everything was different. Time had taken its toll, and people had moved on. Where there were parks were now shops, where there were shops were now homes, and where there were homes were now parks. Even the castle wasn't the same.

I visited one of these parks and sat on a bench.

Even these trees are different.

Then, I noticed a bit of light glint off a large tree near the back. I approached and saw a metal plate embedded in a tree trunk. The trunk had somewhat grown over it, but I was still able to read the familiar Aleurian characters.

Necromancer's Folly

> This tree is dedicated to Wolfram Arthur Tors who passed this year, IC 208.
> By decree of Lord Arthur Edgar Tors, this tree shall stand for all time.

For the first time in a while, my emotions were a little more present as tears began to form in the corner of my eyes. I placed my hand on the tree and felt a sense of peace. This tree was dedicated to my grandfather by my uncle, and it had stood there ever since.

"Maybe not everything has changed," I smiled to myself.

I could feel my dulled sense of depression wash away as all the colors of the world felt just a little more vibrant.

A branch snapped behind me and I turned to look.

Approaching me were the familiar faces of Reginald and Myrril, a look of concern plastered on their faces.

"Oh, hey. Where did you come from?" I asked.

"W-We followed you..." Myrril sheepishly stated.

Reginald spoke up, "Are you okay? We've been concerned about you ever since the tomb."

I nodded, then turned back to the tree, "I'm doing much better now. Thank you for your concern."

"We knocked o-on your door every day, but you never answered," Myrril said.

"I'm sorry. I didn't want to see anyone."

"We get that," Reginald said, "We were just concerned is all."

"And um..." Reginald looked at Myrril, then back at me,

Epilogue

"I need to ask you something." He took a deep breath, "Who are you, really?"

I stayed silent while processing his question, but he continued to speak.

"When we first met, you killed a direwolf in one swing. Then you asked a ton of weird questions that you should have already known. I didn't think it was weird at the time, but then more things happened."

"When we were in the sewers, you acted like you could see in the dark," He continued, "The wound you took on the arm was miraculously not as bad as it was a moment before, then you took a direct hit from one of the big husks and then got up like it was nothing!"

"Khris took the s-same hit and he almost d-died!" Myrril added.

"Yeah, and there's even more," Reginald kept going, "When we were searching for the tomb, you seemed to be pushing us in the right direction the whole time, and then you seemed to be able to read the words above the entrance. Inside, you freaked out more than everyone else when we saw Draugr. You froze up and we thought you died. Then your eyes glowed and you cast some crazy spell that killed them all."

Wait, my eyes glowed? I don't remember that happening.

"I was able to accept most of what had happened, but then even *more* happened!" He added, "We ended up fighting Lost Light and I saw you moving crazy fast. Not to mention you were covered in blood but didn't have a single scratch on you!"

"Then, that Lich recognized you and you called him your uncle, which should be impossible, but you even have the same last name. You even pushed us away without saying anything. Then, when we came back, you were talking to him as he died and even seemed ready to cry over him!"

Reginald was breathing heavily as he was trying to say all of that before I responded, not knowing I was going to let him speak.

"So I'll ask one more time. Who are you?" He said again.

Both of them were looking at me expectantly as I contemplated my next action.

Reginald is more perceptive than I gave him credit for.

I let out a heavy sigh as I came to a decision.

"I haven't been honest with you," I started, "My name is Elric Wolfram Tors."

I took a deep breath.

"I'm an Aleurian."

A Throne Room – Elsewhere in the world.

Rows of finely armored individuals, carrying masterfully made pikes designed as if they grew from nature itself, lined the walls of an extravagant audience hall; Its tall roof supported my numerous tree-shaped pillars which sprawled out to create a stone canopy across the tall ceiling.

At the end of the chamber was a grand domed alcove with crystal clear windows set above in such a way as to always direct sunlight upon the opulent throne of golden bark that stood beneath.

Seated upon the throne was a man with long golden hair, cerulean blue eyes, and elongated ears that came to a point. Fine clothing the color of grass and interwoven with golden

Epilogue

thread covered the man's lithe form. The snow-white circlet upon his head dazzled with brilliance and entranced all those who saw it.

"My daughter. The time has come for you to be of use," The man spoke with an almost crystalline voice that carried with it a tone of disappointment and apprehension.

Kneeling before the throne was a beautiful woman with equally golden hair and lapis-colored eyes. Her ears came to a long point and bent slightly outward, the same as the man on the throne.

The man on the throne continued to speak, "Against my better judgment, it has been decided that you shall meet with our brethren who gather within the Great Forest of Aryl'lin. It will be your duty to aid them in their struggle."

"Yes, Father," The woman responded with a slightly shaky voice.

"I do not believe you are worthy of such a task," The man sneered, "However, with your siblings busy on other fronts, there is no choice. Do not disappoint me."

Those last words were said with such force that it sent chills down the spines of even the royal guard.

"I-I will not, Father," The woman managed to stammer.

"I doubt that very much," The man scoffed, "Now, begone. You leave tomorrow at dawn."

GLOSSARY

Abnormal – An Unnatural Creature not of this world, occasionally twisted and mutated Beasts. Often times the line between Beast and Abnormal blurs, as such the Abnormal is defined as a creature that cannot naturally reproduce.

Aleuria – An Island off the coast of Vestri. It was once home to the Aleurian People, during which time it got its name. After their downfall, it was renamed to Alurland over time.

Aleurian – The People of the Island of Aleuria. One of the Elder Races, the first races to appear. The Aleurians were often said to have "The cunning of the Dwarves, the magic of the Elves, and the strength of the Giants". They died out over eleven hundred years prior to the story. Elric is seemingly the last of his kind. They have an average lifespan of 120 years.

Aleurian Empire – The nation of the Aleurian People whose history spans over eight thousand years. It once controlled all of Vestri, as well as some of Nordri and Sudri.

Glossary

Association/The Wensworth Association for Wayward Souls – A mercenary organization that covers all of Vestri, the Western Continent. They are not a mercenary company but are instead closer to information brokers and job screeners.

Association Medal – The Association Medal is a form of Identification and a way for employers to know that you are reliable. The image on the front of the Medal shows how highly the Association ranks your skills based on the historical abilities of all of its members over the past several centuries. The back contains information about who you are, and the completion rate of the jobs you have accepted through the Association.

Atre – Lord and Ruler of Kyrtvale.

Beast – A natural-born creature who cannot be labeled as a normal animal. Many times Beasts are mixed up with Abnormals, in such a case a Beast is defined as a creature that can naturally reproduce.

Beastfolk – Beastfolk are, for lack of a better term, Humanoid Animals; Humanoid Land Mammals to be exact. They often have abilities that surpass those of a Human, and as such they were persecuted for a very long period of time. However, if one were to close their eyes and have a conversation with a Beastfolk, they would be indistinguishable from a human.

Bloodstone – A natural stone of condensed Megin found deep within the earth. They can hold a tremendous amount of magical energy, like a magic battery, and are often used as a spellcasting focus to aid mages. In the past, the Aleurians knew that Bloodstones were notoriously difficult to manage, and only the most talented, or the craziest, ever

Glossary

used one to amplify their Megin. It is named for its deep crimson color.

Continents – The Western Continent is named Vestri, the Northern is Nordri, the Eastern is Austri, and the southern is Sudri.

Direwolf – A Beast that is much larger than a normal Wolf and sports bone-like armor on its arms, shoulders, and back. They are known to lead packs of normal wolves and other direwolves. They come in an equal number of variants as there are regular wolves.

Draugr – Sentinels who guard ancient tombs even in death. They have shrunken, mummified skin and carry the arms and armor they were buried with. Often seen as a myth to scare away grave robbers.

Dragon – An encompassing term to describe large reptilian beasts. They were romanticized as the king of beasts during the Dragon Hunting craze during the Aleurian Middle Kingdom Era (Roughly four thousand years before the fall). Some examples of a Dragon include the Drake, the Wyrm, and the Lindworm. Wyverns are considered Lesser Dragons and are often not referred to by the term "Dragon".

Dwarf – They have a shorter and broader stature than a human, with round faces and large eyes. They are known for their massive underground fortresses and unmatched technological innovation. They have an average lifespan of 300 years. One of the Elder Races.

Dvergen Steel – Steel made using the dwarven technique. It is known for its greater transfer of Megin through the metal as well as its increased strength against sheering forces. It was once the go-to metal for weaponry.

Edren – A city in the center of the Eye of the

Continent. It was once a human village that was taken by the Aleurian Empire and transformed into a central powerhouse of the region. In current times, it serves as the central hub for trade between several large kingdoms and as the current seat of power for the Valtion-Silma City State Alliance.

Elder Race – The oldest and most powerful of the races on Talmara. They were the first to inhabit the planet. They consist of the Aleurians, the Elves, the Dwarves, and the Giants.

Elf – Normally indistinguishable from humans beyond the pointed ears and long lifespan. Elves are experts in Megin manipulation and Magecraft. They have two types; the Common Elf, and the High Elf. When people say "Elf" they most often refer to the Common Elf. High Elves are the Elvish royalty and have unconfirmed life spans, however it is said that the current elvish king has been around for more than five millennia. The average lifespan of a Common Elf is 400 years. One of the Elder Races.

Elfbane – A slur used by Elves to describe the Humans of the Faeron Kingdom who overthrew their ancestors and enslaved their people even to this day.

Einheri – Nickname given to General Wolfram Arthur Tors. Meaning, "The one man army".

Etterkommer – Meaning descendant. Used to refer to people descended from Aleurian blood. These people are more powerful than the average human, but fall far short of the power of the Aleurians.

Eye of the Continent – The valley situated between the Serpents Crest Mountains. When viewed on a map, the area resembles an eye.

Faerium Steel – Steel made using Elvish techniques.

It has the highest Megin transfer of all other steel types and has the advantage of being lighter and more flexible as well. However, the lessened weight often makes it less effective as a battlefield weapon.

Grell – Small nuisance creatures with a high rate of population, similar to Coyote's in that aspect. They are about the size of a dog with six legs and a face that looks as though someone mixed a bat and a hog, then curb-stomped it and gave it rabies.

Grimwa – The small Imp-like creature that works as Lord Atre's assistant.

Half Elf – A mixed race individual crossed between an Elf and a Human. They have an increased lifespan of close to 200 years.

Half Orc – A mixed-race individual crossed between an Orc and a Human. They often take more traits from their Orc parent than their Human parent but tend to have a more human-like appearance.

Husk – The corpse of a Human, devoid of its soul, who wanders mindlessly on pure instinct. Until recently, they were only naturally created by pooling Megin and the result was a fairly weak individual. However, a new type of Husk has emerged as the result of Koberic's unnatural experiments.

Kyrtvale – The Afterlife; the Underworld. The place where the soul goes after death. For some it is paradise, for others; a punishment. Often referred to as "The Vale" and used as substitution for the world "Hell" in several expressions. For example, "What the hell?" would be "What in Kyrtvale?" or simply "What the Vale?"

Glossary

Lich – An undead mage that retains its former intelligence, personality, and abilities.

Lizardfolk – Lizardfolk are sometimes described as "Human Sized Lizards that walk on their hind legs", and nothing is more accurate. Like Beastfolk, they often have abilities that differ, or are superior, to human abilities. However, also like Beastfolk, their mental facilities are indistinguishable from humans.

Mage – The ancient term meant "A person who uses magic". However, the modern meaning is "A person who uses spells".

Magic – The manipulation of Megin to create or modify natural and unnatural phenomena.

Megin – The lifeblood of the universe, a type of energy that flows through all living and non-living things.

Orc – A nomadic race of people. They have greenish-grey skin, tusks, and natural chitinous armor around their arms, legs, and vitals. Their intelligence is indistinguishable from a human.

Serpents Crest Mountains – A tall range of mountains that encircles a valley nearly five hundred miles in diameter.

Silverfang Timberlands – The forest that takes up most of the Eye of the Continent. Home to a vast variety of dangerous Beasts, the most abundant being wolves and direwolves. Named after a famous silver Direwolf, Silverfang, nearly 800 years prior to the story.

Spell – A magical equation used to create the exact same effect each time. Uses Megin gathered from the surroundings as its energy source.

Glossary

Sorcerer – A magic user who uses the Megin within their own body to cast magic. Very rare to see a human Sorcerer due to their low amount of internal Megin.

Solaire – The currency of the Aleurian Empire. Came in three types of coin; Gold, Silver, and Bronze.

Sovereign – The official currency of the western continent, it was introduced by the Dolar Imperium and eventually spread to all the other nations on Vestri, even those who dislike the Imperium. They come in three kinds of coin; Gold, Silver, and Copper.

Talmara – The name of the World in which the story takes place.

Tomb of the Fallen – A tomb found in every Aleurian city used to house the bodies of fallen warriors.

Valtion-Silma City State Alliance – An alliance of city states that spans the Eye of the Continent. The members consist of Leindale, Roswin, Dancastle, Edren, Onforde, Torrel, and Mellgarde. The current chairman of the Alliance is Edren.

The Gods
The Elder Gods:

Aleura – Goddess of Creation and Order. She was heavily worshiped by the Aleurian people, whom they named themselves after. The Opposite of Njordurn; Order cannot exist without chaos.

Njordurn – God of Destruction and Chaos. The opposite of Aleura, but acknowledged as a required force. Chaos cannot exist without Order.

Glossary

The Patron Gods; The Thirteen:

Murmanus – God of earth and stone and the patron of miners and Dwarves; all that happens within the dirt is his domain.

Oceanis – Goddess of the sea and patron of sailors. She is both kind and fair, yet her temper is the fear of all men.

Polimus – God of life, protector of the forests, and Patron of healers.

Ormr – God of Beasts, Patron of huntsmen and herders. He is seen as the progenitor of all beasts.

Duruna – God of Time, Keeper of the Sands, Lord of the Hourglass. The Unbiased God.

Tors – God of Craftsmen and Storms, Patron of all those who work with their hands.

Jurian – God of Wisdom and Knowledge, Patron to scholars.

Verona – Goddess of Hearth and Home, Patron God of families.

Famir – God of Agriculture, Patron of farmers.

Elena – Goddess of Love and Emotion, Patron of young men and women. She is known to toy with the emotions of the young. Married to the God of War.

Khrom – God of War. Armies pray to him before battle, and rulers consult with his priests before war.

Emmerich – God of Travelers and Tradesmen, Patron of Merchants, and those who travel along the roads.

Aegar – God of Megin and Magic, Patron of Magic-Users and worshipped by the Elves.

The Cardinal Gods:

Glossary

Noth – God of the Northern Winds, a white bear in the deep north

Sao – God of the Southern Winds, a tri-tailed scorpion of the scorching deserts

Erst – God of the Eastern Winds, a majestic stag of the old forests.

Wern – God of the Western Winds, an eagle soaring in the far skies.

Association Ranks

Væng – The first and lowest rank. It's given to everyone who signs up with the association and is represented by the symbol of a single folded wing. Also called Rookies, these people make up around thirteen percent of members.

Fella Væng – The second rank. Represented by two folded wings, these Novices make up nearly twenty-four percent of members.

Svífa Væng – The third rank makes up close to thirty-nine percent of members and is represented by two open wings.

Örn – The fourth rank. If you manage to make it to this point, you are considered an expert by the Association. This is represented by a flying eagle and makes up about nineteen percent of members.

Stjarna Örn – The fifth rank. Most people cannot achieve this rank because of their own physical limitations. Hiring someone of this rank costs an extraordinary amount of wealth and they are highly sought after by kingdoms wishing to keep them on retainer in case of invasion. They are represented by a soaring eagle with one star underneath and they make up about three percent of members.

Skínandi Örn – The sixth and final rank. These people are few and far between, with only three appearing in the last few centuries. These living legends are represented by a soaring eagle with two stars underneath. If you ever meet one, you would either be the luckiest or the unluckiest person in the world.

ABOUT THE AUTHOR

Drew R. Stowell was born and raised in southern California where he is the second of three children. He maintains a close relationship with his family and enjoys assisting his grandparents and spending quality time with them.

From a young age, Drew exhibited an imagination that surpassed that of his peers, which he channeled into his writing. His debut novel, *Necromancer's Folly*, showcases his creative prowess and marks the beginning of his journey as an author.